Emily Black put her life on hold to look after her difficult elderly mother. On the southwest coast of England, one of the highlights of Emily's week is when she goes to buy coffee, where she quietly flirts with a shamelessly sexy and attractive barista. After an unexpected encounter during a night out, Emily discovers her nameless barista is the enigmatic Gabriel Hunter-Law. Gabriel, from an infamous wealthy family, has a reputation of being a heartless playboy millionaire and notorious bachelor.

On impulse, Gabriel offers Emily a place to stay for the week to avoid her brother's imminent visit, because he would like to get to know her better. Although initially shocked by the suggestion, Emily accepts. They quickly end up in a passionate, physical relationship. As events in both their worlds collide, Emily discovers the dark secrets Gabriel hides, which ultimately may be the reason they cannot be together. Is their bond strong enough to fight for a happy ending, or will the ghosts from the past, which Gabriel obsessively tries to conceal, succeed in tearing them apart?

One Week
Copyright © 2020 Floella Ingram
ISBN: 978-1-4874-3073-3
Cover art by Martine Jardin

Published by eXtasy Books Inc or
Devine Destinies, an imprint of eXtasy Books Inc

Look for us online at:
www.eXtasybooks.com or www.devinedestinies.com

One Week
Hunter-Law 1

By

Floella Ingram

DEDICATION

For M.

CHAPTER ONE

L ate. Horribly, inexcusably late. I move in a half-run, clutching my mother's shopping. The heavens open, and it starts to rain. Heavy rain. Hard penetrating rain, which soaks me quickly. My feet slip in my sandals, slowing my pace. I watch everyone around me dart towards the nearest shelter or retrieve umbrellas and hurriedly put on rain macs. The most I can do is pull my arms around me over my blouse, as if this will somehow shield me from the relentless water. I drag my hair back into a loose ponytail so it is not dripping around my face like seaweed.

My mother will be furious, but there is no way around it. I stop outside the coffee shop for the last items on the list, pulling the push door as I always do and stumbling inside.

It's empty. There is none of the usual background chatter, just the low whirring of a fan on the counter. The bleached wood benches are tidy and scrubbed clean, the lunchtime rush long since ended. No one stands at the counter as I squelch towards it, my sandals slapping inelegantly against the stone floor. He appears from the kitchen, the man I have been quietly flirting with and secretly crushing on for the last few months, since I came home to look after my mother. I exchange snippets of conversation with him about the weather, the flower market, world news, and my mother's health. Every time, I dream of a deeper conversation, but I am under no illusion it will happen. I know virtually nothing about him. He always turns the conversation back to me. It makes me feel special and less invisible than I usually do.

Good customer service, I guess. I do not even know his name, but he always smiles. His smile lights up his entire face as his warm brown eyes twinkle mischievously. He is tall, broad, and tanned with high cheekbones and light stubble. His dark brown hair is sun-kissed and outgrown from a shorter traditional style, long and floppy on top but brushed back from his face. He looks like he has just stepped out of a magazine or off a surfboard.

I do not kid myself there is anything in this. He is undeniably gorgeous. I see the way other women swoon and hang on his every word while buying deli treats and sandwiches, women far more alluring and attractive than me. Still, he brightens my day, even for the briefest of moments. Except for today. Today I resemble a drowned rat. I inwardly curse that he is in. He is not always. I assume he is part time, studying maybe or something. I have no idea how old he is, but I guess maybe late twenties. He seems far too confident and self-assured to be younger.

He smiles when he sees me. Then frowns, looking slightly amused. "No coat?" His voice is husky and deep, lips full and inviting to be kissed.

I flush and hesitate to answer, feeling the colour rush to my cheeks. "N-no, I-I didn't see the weather forecast." Not very imaginative, but true. I rarely get time to catch up on such things, and my mother is permanently glued to the cookery channels.

He smiles again. "Storm Olivia from the Caribbean or somewhere."

The fan turns towards me. The breeze hits me, and I shiver as the air moves through my wet blouse. I squirm awkwardly under the intensity of his gaze while trying to locate a coherent thought.

He strokes his fingers along the counter in front of me, frowning once more. "Wait there."

He disappears into the back of the shop. The fitted black t-shirt he is wearing and tight black jeans cling to his frame and accentuate his muscles. He comes back and places a fawn coloured jumper on the counter with an expensive looking man's umbrella. I stand motionless, not understanding.

"You're cold, and it's tipping down," he explains plainly.

I realise he means to lend them to me. I feel shy and stupid. "Oh, no. I couldn't."

He raises an eyebrow. "I trust you to give them back. Anyway, your shirt's gone see-through, it's so wet. Much as I am enjoying the view, I don't suppose it was the look you were going for when you left your house this morning."

His voice is unusually commanding as he runs his eyes down to my chest. I follow his eyes with mine, horrified. He is right. My blouse is clinging to me and completely transparent. You can see my breasts fighting to escape my bra. Worse still, my nipples are hard as bullets from the cold and pushing through the lace. My only saving thought is he at least cannot see my bra has gone slightly grey from over washing. I chastise myself instantly for thinking he would be remotely interested in my bra. I know without looking my cheeks are bright red. I stand there utterly mortified. Defeated, I reach for the jumper. There is a pause. A moment of silence cackles between us with an unexplained intensity.

He smiles kindly and breaks it with his sympathy. "The usual?"

I nod feebly, feeling even more awkward. The jumper is soft. Cashmere, I think. The tag reads Hugo Boss, which surprises me for someone who works sporadically in a coffee shop. I do not know why it bothers me. Maybe it was a gift. I watch him froth the milk as I pull the jumper over my head. It is too big for me, but it is warm and comforting. It smells fresh and vaguely of sandalwood. I breathe deeply, and the scent fills my senses. I imagine it is how he smells. He places the hot chocolate with marshmallows and a sticky bun on the counter in front of me. Salted caramel muffin on this occasion. I hand him the money, and he grazes his fingers across my palm as he gives me my change. A shot of electricity sears through me at the contact. Did he mean to do that? Why would he? I am such an idiot, and I know I am blushing after the merest touch like a schoolgirl again. Feeling exposed once more, I thank him hurriedly while darting out of the shop. I can still feel his eyes trained on me, as I step back into the pouring rain.

CHAPTER TWO

I turn the key in the lock with trepidation. I know what is coming.

We have arranged for a hospital bed to be put in the lounge, which is where my mother lives pretty much now. Her voice rasps and clips from the lounge. "Emily? Emily is that you?"

"Yes, Mum. It's me."

I look in on her from around the door. In leopard print leggings and a chestnut coloured brown top, she is propped up in bed on the many cushions. The food network channel is murmuring in the background. I hurriedly take off my sandals, still wet from the rain, walking barefoot into the lounge to face the inevitable.

"You're late. I'm wasting away."

She is cross, which I had expected. The empty lunch dishes from her lunchtime home care visit are on the table beside her. She narrows her eyes to scrutinise me. "That's not your jumper."

I shrug self-consciously, not wanting this conversation. Instead, I put her shopping on the sofa, ignoring her statement. "I brought your favourite." I remove the dishes and move the table back over to her. Then I place the sticky bun and hot chocolate well within her reach.

She says nothing as she reaches for a knife to cut the bun into quarters, which she devours greedily. The cream surrounds her mouth and merges with her lipstick before she daps it away with a serviette.

She focuses her eyes on me once more. "I need you to dye my hair this evening. My roots are showing."

I cannot in all honesty see a single root or hair out of place, but my mother is uncompromising in her appearance. "I can't, Mum, not tonight. It's Lucy's hen party, and I'm the designated driver."

She frowns and huffs. "Leaving me to fend for myself," she snaps.

"No, of course not. Cynthia is coming over."

"Cynthia?"

"From the church. Your friend."

She huffs again. "No friend of mine. Geriatric busy body-ing do-gooder. Fine, go out, but try to make some effort with your appearance. It's not as if anyone is likely to show any interest in you looking like that. When I was your age, I was fighting them off with a stick."

I pick up the dishes. There is little point in retaliating. "I'm going to wash the dishes and get things ready for Cynthia this evening."

She does not reply. As I leave the room, I hear the TV volume go up once more. I feel guilty, which I know is silly, but I feel guilty anyway. She is terminally ill and not much past sixty. This is the second time I have gone out since I came back nine months ago to care for her. I gave up everything I had started to create as my own life after graduating. My apartment. My temping job at the British archives whilst I studied for a master's in literature and art history. My freedom. Even my cat, who my boss had generously adopted.

It was not a choice. I knew I had to do it, in an overwhelming sense of duty and responsibility I do not feel bitter about. I do, though, admit to moments of regret and frustration for everything I have left behind. Without live-in care, she would be in a home or a hospice, something she has always stated adamantly will never happen. I do not even expect her to be grateful, but she takes great delight in constantly criticising and venting her frustrations on me. I used to argue back and challenge it, which only serves to make her more venomous. It is easier to just ignore it. She resents being ill, and she resents me for not being ill. If nothing else, as the cancer consumes her slowly, she resents me for not living in the way she would choose. Our relationship is no less strained or chastising than it has always been and intensified in her eyes. It's ironic. Her whole life she has always wanted to be the centre of the party and the attention. Now that she finally is, she cannot bear it.

We have carers who come in four times a day, but the rest is up to me. The nights are the worst. She chooses to sleep more in the day, which increases her needs through the twilight hours. She knows how to play me. She knows the guilt will eat me up if I do not bend to her constant demands and instructions. I know this is not forever, but increasingly, I wonder how much of me will be left at the end, which makes me feel even worse. I never wanted her to feel like she is a burden to me, even though she is.

I help at Lucy's floristry shop twice a week, which is my escape and gives me a small allowance. Lucy is my best friend from school and my rock. She gets married next month to Rob, the boy we went to school with, who lived next door. I am happy for them. Really happy for them, though it highlights everything lacking in my own life. They make such a perfect couple and family with their three-year-old son, Noah. True soulmates who know each other inside out.

We're having an early hen do because Rob is going away for his stag to Dublin and Lucy has several weekend floristry jobs before the big day. Lucy has also joked it will give everyone time to recover. She anticipates a boozy affair. Not for me, though. I have volunteered to be the designated driver. Clubbing is not really my thing.

I finish counting my mother's various tablets into an eggcup and hear her ringing her bell. By seven, I have managed to have a quick shower. I look at myself in the mirror. It is not a nightclubbing dress. It is too long and too flowery, but it gives me the illusion of having curves in the right places and flashes a reasonable amount of cleavage. Hopefully I might at least manage to blend in and not look like I am dressed for traffic court.

I am wearing my hair down in an attempt to look like I have made more of an effort. Unfortunately, the more I brush it, the more my hair seems determined to curl and kink in all the wrong directions. I apply some makeup without any real precision and a red lipstick which makes me look like a cheap painted doll. When I attempt to wipe it from my lips with a tissue, the colour seems remarkably resilient.

The doorbell rings. It is Cynthia. She is wearing a wool suit in the same iron grey colour as her hair with a bulbous necklace of turquoise plastic. She shuffles in and hangs up her coat while I hold her knitting bag.

"You look nice, dear," she mutters without looking at me.

"Thank you for sitting with Mum tonight." I am genuinely grateful and try to convey how much in my voice.

She bustles past me into the lounge. "No problem. You should be getting out at your age. You don't want to get left on the shelf."

My mother has heard everything, despite claiming to not hear well. She looks me up and down with her critical, beady eyes. "She's not going to find anyone looking like that. You're not going to a church fete, are you?"

Cynthia looks at me with sympathy. "It's a pretty dress, Grace."

My mother snorts. "If she was middle aged and not making much effort after having children."

As I look down at my dress, the heat rises in my cheeks.

Admittedly, it is not the most exciting dress or particularly suited for a nightclub, but it is not completely awful. With no time to change and nothing more suitable to change into, I head for the door.

As I approach Lucy's front door, which is festooned with pink balloons and a large blow up penis, I feel even more unsuitably dressed. I take a deep breath and let myself in. There are eight of us in total. I do not really know the others more than to say hello. Lucy's mother is the other designated driver, but she is not staying. She's meeting a friend for a late supper. We are going to a new nightclub in Plymouth, down by the harbour, called *Incubus*. A reportedly exclusive and expensive affair which also features a restaurant, private members club, and spa. I am not sure we are going to get there in reality. Everyone is already a little more than tipsy on tequila shots, but by nine-thirty, we are on the road.

Lucy loops her arm in mine as we walk along the promenade. Her hands are cold, and she towers over me in her stiletto sandals.

"You look pretty tonight." Her voice is slightly slurring.

I raise an eyebrow in response.

It seems to amuse her as she giggles. "Okay, so it's not really a clubbing dress, but you do look pretty."

I meet her eyes with mine. I do not argue. I can tell she means it despite my reservations.

She squeezes my arm. "Thanks again for driving. I wish I'd said no when you offered. You could have let your hair down and had some fun."

"It's fine. It will be fun anyway," I lie unconvincingly, and we do not talk any further.

9

CHAPTER THREE

Incubus is a huge building with long black windows and a dark façade. The entrance is flanked by many bouncers with headsets and stern expressions. The inside is equally dark and intimidating, but with soft lighting which provides pools of light in the darkness. Huge floor to ceiling fish tanks line the entrance corridor filled with black and silver fish. We walk down a few stairs into a large open space to numerous booths off to the sides with black padded seating and slick, shiny tables. The music is floaty and ambient, accompanied by a low, murmuring beat. A huge bar crosses the entire back wall. Bottles of multi-coloured liquids fill the shelves and reflect the lights like a kaleidoscope.

I want to hate it, but I don't. I do, though, feel increasingly out of place. It's busy, but the room gives the illusion of space. A space filled with lots of beautiful people. Leggy blondes in tight fitting dresses, talking to model-standard men in fitted shirts and designer jeans.

Our party quickly settle into a booth and start sampling the cocktails Incubus has already gained quite a reputation for with a price tag to match. After a brief episode of dancing, where I manage to stay mainly hidden in the shadows, I become designated drink and bag watcher. I watch the other girls come and go. Two are busy chatting to guys they have met on the dancefloor. The others continually refill Lucy's glass, which empties at an alarming rate, although she appears to be holding her own.

I play with the straw in my lemonade, stabbing the lime

slice, and fleetingly wonder if I should have brought a book to read. That is when I feel it, an unexplainable feeling of being watched. I look up and see a man at the bar. He locks his gaze onto mine. Eyes which are penetrating and unforgiving. His lips are set in a grim line. He looks strangely familiar, but I have no idea where I could have met him. He is strikingly gorgeous, with chiselled features and olive skin, light stubble, and intimidating in the way he holds himself. His expression is cold and imposing. A true alpha male, even at this distance. He looks expensive, dressed in a black shirt and jacket with dark jeans. His hair looks dark brown or black in the dim light, casually brushed back from his face.

A very attractive and tall blonde girl is draped around him like a scarf, laughing into her phone. He cannot be looking at me. I look around, but there is no one else there as he continues to hold me in place with the intensity of his stare. Then he smiles that smile, the one which lights up his entire face. I know then this is the boy from the coffee shop, looking nothing like a boy and like I have never seen him before. He shrugs, which causes his companion to slink away. She is obviously disgruntled as he walks in my direction, ignoring whatever she is saying to him as he leaves. I shuffle uncomfortably in my seat as he stands by the table.

"Hey, nice surprise. I wouldn't have expected to see you here. Didn't think this was your sort of thing?"

I look up and our eyes meet. His voice is far more assertive than I remember it. I feel myself blush. Of course, I must stick out like a sore thumb. "It's my best friend's hen party. I'm the designated driver," I squeak.

He smiles at me once more, sensing my unease, I think.

"Oh, that makes sense. I meant not your thing in a good way." He continues to stare at me, which does not help. "What do you think of the place?"

I relax slightly. "It's very tasteful and not as crowded as I expected. Expensive, though."

He grins slightly. "You think it's expensive?"

"Yes, hideously so. Don't you?"

"You should tell the owner. He would welcome the feedback." His grin widens, as he avoids the question.

I roll my eyes. "I doubt it. I imagine he's probably some bimbo-obsessed semi-gangster wannabe. Are you here with friends?" I glance over at the blonde, who is still glaring at us. Well, glaring at me, specifically.

He does not look around, still grinning, but biting his bottom lip now as if he is trying not to laugh. "Is that not a little stereotyped? No, not with friends. I'm working. Well, supposedly."

This catches me off guard. I feel myself tense again, instantly regretting my earlier comments. "Oh, so what do you do here?" Maybe this explains why he is not always at the shop.

"I own the place, like the coffee shop. I've been there more than I would normally be for the last few months since we opened. It's a new set up and team. I've been helping them all settle in. I like going back to the floor, so to speak." He pauses, watching me flounder in my own embarrassment, continuing to scrutinise me with his eyes. "You look surprised."

"I just didn't expect it." My words choke out. Surprised would be an understatement.

He smiles, but his expression is unreadable and distant. "People are generally not what they seem, in my experience." Without warning, he outstretches his hand. "Come on. I'll give you a tour of the building."

He continues to hold out his hand, observing me curiously. I feel the colour increase in my cheeks again. My anxiety rises. I feel ridiculous for allowing him to have this impact on me.

"I can't," I blurt. "I have to stay here to watch the bags and drinks."

He looks amused once more and gestures to a huge bouncer at the side of the room, who immediately joins us. Tall, and muscle bound, he is dressed all in black with a shaven head, which makes him look even more severe. He looks ex-military as he stands awaiting instructions, almost as if he is standing to attention.

"Felix, will you watch these ladies' things until we get back." His tone is commanding and low. There is no hint of the soft huskiness I have grown accustomed to whilst buying coffee.

Felix nods quickly. "Yes, of course, sir."

He outstretches his hand once more, and I have nowhere left to hide. I take it, like Alice falling down the rabbit hole. His skin is smooth and warm. The cold metal of the ring on his thumb brushes against my palm. I shudder as a pulse of electricity moves through me. I meet his gaze with my own, and he smiles in response. I wonder if he feels it, too.

CHAPTER FOUR

The Incubus building is truly impressive. He explains it is not completely finished yet, as we take the lift between the floors. The second and third floors are an extension of the club. They are unified and connected by a series of transparent staircases which look as though they are floating in the air. The fourth floor is a private members club, elegant and almost baroque in style with leather armchairs and pretty hostesses in short, fitted black dresses. The fifth floor is a restaurant which specialises in local seafood and steak. He explains he is trying to recreate the quality of steak you can get in New York and has been working with a local farmer and butcher on different cuts and cattle breeds. It all smells divine and is buzzing with what looks to be mainly prominent figures and personalities from the area, who I recognise from pictures in the local papers. The sixth floor is a spa which is closed, so we do not stay long. I am struck by a huge painting of the ocean in reception. The artist's initials are GH which means nothing to me. It is a stunning piece of work, stormy and atmospheric.

He talks with excitement about the building, obviously proud of what he has created. Everywhere people stare at us, from the staff to the customers. It makes me increasingly anxious, and I feel like one of the fish in the many tanks. If he notices, he does not comment. We reach the seventh floor and step into an empty foyer. It is softly lit with light wooden flooring and panoramic windows which reach from the floor to the ceiling. I can see the lights in the harbour below. The view stretches across the entire sound.

"So, this is my floor. It's not finished, but I have an office up here and the makings of a spare apartment," he explains.

I walk over to the window, wondering briefly what a spare apartment would be used for. "The view is incredible."

I can feel him behind me, very close behind me.

"Yes, it is," he replies.

I turn and see just how close he is. Our bodies are almost touching. Reaching his hand to my face and into my hair, he pushes his lips to mine, hard and urgent. I readily respond. He loops his hands around my waist and explores my mouth with a veracity and hunger. I flatten my back against the cold glass of the window. He tastes of brandy and smells of the sandalwood mixed with lime from his jumper. I feel out of my depth, like I am in some sort of surreal dream. Bringing my arms up around his shoulders, I find the soft hair at the nape of his neck with my fingers. Penetrating my mouth with his tongue, he pulls me closer into him. He moves his hands down my back until both rest on my bottom.

Our bodies feel like they are moulding into one as we press into each other. My heart races. He lifts one of my legs up and wraps it around him. Moving his hands under my dress and stroking his fingers up my thighs, he kneads the soft flesh of my buttocks. His hands move to the side, and he loops his fingers around the fabric of my knickers. I freeze. I am clear on his intention and want it badly, but I am equally shy about what will happen next.

He pulls his mouth from mine, his cheeks slightly flushed. His hands remain on my hips, tangled in my knickers. "Are you okay?" His voice is husky, and his eyes are slightly hooded.

I am not sure I can speak. "Yes," I finally manage. My voice sounds alien to me like it belongs to someone else. "I'm just not used to . . ."

"Used to fucking nightclub owners the first night you meet

them?" He concludes my sentence for me. His bluntness shocks me. His eyes do not leave mine. They are carnal and slightly wild. "This again is a good thing, and why I find you so attractive. I see so many girls in here drop their knickers for a free drink or whatever without even being asked. Actually, the boys aren't much better, from what I've seen."

He finds me attractive. I try to process his words, finding it impossible to concentrate on anything with him so close to me. I am also very aware, from what he has just said, that he is not lacking in female attention and what he is currently doing is probably a fairly common occurrence.

"I'm sorry. I usually have more restraint. I shouldn't have assumed you felt the same way, but I've wanted to kiss you for a very long time. You caught me off guard, being here tonight."

He sounds genuinely regretful, and I am unsure if it is me or the situation.

"It-it's fine. It w-was nice," I stutter out.

"Nice?" He raises an eyebrow smiling slightly, clearly amused by my choice of words. "Oh, yes, I can assure you it would be *nice*."

He emphasises the word *nice*. As he does, he unloops his fingers and slowly glides them under the material at the top of my knickers, grazing them across my skin. I shiver. It feels so good. My whole body comes alive with nervous anticipation, a brief escape, as if, for a moment, I am someone else, someone free of cares and responsibilities.

He moves his hands underneath my dress, up my body over the roll of my tummy, which I try not to dwell on. He cups my breasts with his fingers, massaging them through the lacy fabric of my bra. My nipples lengthen and harden under his touch. He fixes his gaze utterly onto mine, putting his hands on my lower back once more, pulling me into him.

"Yes, it would definitely be nice," he murmurs.

Resting his hand under my thigh, he lifts my leg a little higher around him. His erection rubs between my legs while he kisses me again. I push my body tight against the tautness of his. His warmth wraps around me. My nipples are tingling and wanting more.

He pulls his lips away from mine and continues, softly. "I would like to see you again, properly."

I am utterly absorbed by the physical sensation of what he is doing to my body with his. My mind is a swimming soup of confusion. I feel my shyness increase again as he continues to move his body against mine. I'm overwhelmed and unsure now. "I'm not sure it's a good idea. I'm not sure we would be very compatible."

He looks surprised, almost affronted. "Really? That's not what your body is telling me."

He is right. I am aching for him to continue, moving my body shamelessly with his. It is like we are in our own private dance, but I know this is a bad idea.

"I think it's clear we live in different worlds. I don't know, but I'm pretty sure I'm not the kind of girl you usually go for."

He frowns. "How do you mean?"

I blush, not wanting this conversation with him, of all people. How am I supposed to tell him the one serious boyfriend I have ever had was my manipulative childhood sweetheart, and the sex was an utter let down, to put it mildly. In addition, my one night of nearly pity sex with a colleague after a drunk work Christmas party was not my finest moment. To be honest, both encounters have left me wondering what all the fuss is about. With everything that has happened with my mother since, I have had neither the time nor the inclination. This whole situation has disaster written all over it.

"I'm not experienced. I'm sure you've seen a lot more of the world than me." My words rush out. I sound like something out of a Jane Austen novel. Maybe I am being presumptuous, but his earlier comments imply I am not.

He takes a moment to absorb this information and my not very subtle metaphor. His frown deepens. Then he grins. "Seen more of the world? Yes, I've travelled pretty widely."

I shake my head trying not to get lost in the warmth and depth of his eyes. "You know what I mean."

"Yes, I get the point." The grin fades, and he look serious in a flash. "Maybe I read this all wrong, but it felt like you and I have had some sort of connection these last few months."

The heat rises in my cheeks in response. I am utterly transparent. Is it obvious I like him? That I have liked him for all these months, never imagining anything would come of it.

His smile returns, as he continues to hold me against the window with his body. "Well, babe, I'm not looking for experience, if this is what you want?" He continues to hold my eyes with his. His gaze is warm and seductive. His voice is deep and husky.

I nod feebly. My mind is unable to focus on any rational thought. The huge void of loneliness in me is temporarily filled, and my fear of intimacy dissipated. All I want is him. He finds my lips with his, more gently, but his kiss is much deeper as he rubs against me. I respond accordingly, desperate to feel the friction of his jeans against my clitoris. His erection strains beneath the fabric as he continues to explore my body with his hands.

Everything between my legs clenches and throbs while he continues to explore my mouth with his tongue. I explode into an aching climax, unable to contain it any longer. It is almost painful in its intensity. The sensation subsides gradually, leaving my whole body warm and tingling with a sense of lightness.

He slows his pace, his touch gently caressing and soothing. He runs his tongue over my bottom lip. I look down, mortified. The bulge in his trousers is still clearly evident. I may not have dropped my knickers, literally, but I may as well have.

He raises my face in his hands, searching for my eyes with his. "Don't be embarrassed, babe. Don't ever be embarrassed." He kisses my forehead gently, wrapping his arms around me and just holding us there.

My face falls against his chest as my breathing calms. All I can hear is the distant sound of waves crashing and his heart beating.

Eventually we pull apart, and he hands me what looks like a business card. Black with swirling grey writing. All it says is Gabriel Hunter-Law, with a mobile telephone number and an office number.

"Emily. Emily Black," I return, mortified again—only at this stage we are exchanging names. I try desperately to locate my confident, empowered inner goddess.

"I was serious when I said I would like to see you again, properly." He leans closer and whispers in my ear. "My friends call me Gabe."

I shiver once more as he takes my hand and leads me back to the lift to go downstairs. I step back into the nightclub, in a sort of daze.

"Oh, Em." Lucy steps forward unsteadily. She is wearing L plates and a cheap veil now. "There you are. We were worried."

"That's my fault. I'm sorry I stole your friend." He stands forward from behind me, and I watch all their mouths drop open like fish. "Please allow me to buy you all a drink to apologise." He gestures to the bar.

"Um, thank you. That's very kind." Lucy can barely get the words out, though Gabriel seems not to notice.

He leans into me, whispering in my ear once more. "Call me." In an instant, he is gone.

My cheeks burn hot from the force of everyone staring at me.

"*Oh . . . my . . . God!* I think he's even more gorgeous in the flesh than in his photos. You do know who that is, don't you?" one of the group asks.

"It's Gabriel Hunter-Law." I sound sarcastic without meaning to. The question annoys me, mainly because I only found out his name a few minutes ago. My embarrassment rises again. Until tonight he was the nameless, unobtainable man at the coffee shop, my secret, guilty pleasure.

"You have no idea, do you?" she retorts, equally sarcastically. "Gabriel Hunter-Law from one of the wealthiest families in the country. Old and new money. They have links to the Royal family. Guess Daddy is funding this club. Gabriel has a playboy millionaire reputation for being an eternal bachelor and complete player. He's rarely out of the gossip columns. So how on earth do you know him?"

I have no idea what she is talking about. I am drowning on the spot and wanting the ground to open up and swallow me. If that is who he is, asking how I know him would seem like a fair question. The bartender arrives with a large bottle of champagne and glasses, which distracts everyone again.

"I'm so getting details later," Lucy mutters in my ear as she stumbles towards her glass.

CHAPTER FIVE

"So, have you called him yet?" Lucy does not look up from the bridal bouquet she has been working on for the last hour.

We have been working in the back of the shop for most of the day on wedding flowers for tomorrow. My contribution has been mainly trimming stems and the occasional buttonhole. I am grateful for the job. It gets me out of the house for a couple of days a week and gives me a little income, but I am no florist. Plants do not generally seem to like me. The only houseplant I can sustain is a cactus.

I sigh. "No, I haven't. Why would I?"

After her hangover subsided last weekend, Lucy had interrogated me mercilessly. I had admitted to the kiss in the end, but managed to dodge any further disclosure, though I sense she suspected more.

Lucy sighs. "Christ, Em. Why would you not? It's been six days. What's the matter with you? You like him. He obviously likes you. Plus, he's gorgeous and mega rich. What's not to like?"

I roll my eyes at her and flick a stem across the workbench in her direction. "Guys like that just don't go for girls like me. Besides, he has quite a reputation."

I Googled him. Of course, I Googled him. Page after page of photographs of him falling out of nightclubs and parties around the world with a startling array of women. Pictures of beautiful women, including a handful of well know actresses and models, interspersed with a few articles about his mother's funeral some time ago and how he had not attended.

Lucy sighs again. "Who says? Anyway, you're beautiful inside and out. Sure, he has a reputation, but who knows what's really true? I mean the papers make half that stuff up, right? I couldn't find anything about serious relationships or breakups when I Googled him."

Of course, Lucy has Googled him as well.

"Great. He's probably a complete player and a commitment phobe." I sigh.

"Maybe, but maybe not. Come on, Em. I've never seen you moon over a guy this much, like ever. You have to take a risk sometimes. Hell, it could be fun. Just go in with your eyes open."

I shake my head. "Not going to happen."

"What? You're not even a little intrigued to see where this goes?"

I half-laugh, knowing full well she will not let it go. "I already know where this goes. What? Do you think we're going to ride off into the sunset and live happily ever after?"

She nods. "Well, you might. Stranger things have happened, or it might just be really great sex."

I blush in a wave of heat.

Her grin widens. "Seriously, if you'd said last week, you'd be snogging the face off Gabriel Hunter-Law — or any guy you had just met — I would not have believed you. So, ring him."

She has a point. I would not have believed me, either. I had rehearsed the phone call in my head many times now. "Hi, it's Emily from the coffee shop." "Hi, it's Emily from the club the other night." "Hi, it's Emily who metaphorically dropped her knickers for you the other night." This is the one I keep coming back to. It is not as if he is some sort of Prince Charming coming to rescue me from my ivory tower. It is not as if I need to be rescued. My current situation will not be forever, and I chose it.

"Emily, who metaphorically dropped her knickers." It does not matter how I spin it. I keep coming back to it. I am embarrassed I let things go so far and happen so quickly. Do I regret it? Not the feelings and not him, but certainly in terms of what he must think of me and after his comments about other girls in his club. His words gnaw away at my nagging doubts.

"Earth to Emily." Lucy breaks my chain of thought.

I look up to see her observing me curiously.

"I wouldn't know what to say." It's true. Defeated, I do not know how to get around it.

Lucy slams her secateurs on the counter. "I've had enough of this. Go — Go to the shop now. It will be open. Just."

I start to stack the excuses in my head. "He probably won't be there."

"Maybe not, but he may well be. So, go."

Before I can argue any further, I am walking down the hill towards his shop.

Chapter Six

As I reach the door to the coffee shop, my heart is pounding in my ears. My mouth is dry, so dry, my throat hurts. My palms are clammy with sweat. I feel ridiculous. I do not normally react like this. What is it about this man? I curse inwardly. As I walk in, it occurs to me they are about to close in fifteen minutes. The shop is deserted of customers and staff. It is silent and devoid of the usual ambient background jazz, like the last time I was in here. I convince myself he will not be there. It almost works until he walks in from the kitchen.

He stops when he sees me, like he is surprised. Then he frowns, striding forward until he is behind the counter in front of me. His posture is tense. His jaw is tight, and his shoulders are hunched forward. He outstretches his hands on the metal countertop in front of me. The tension cackles almost tangibly, verging on hostility between us.

"You didn't call. Did you lose my number?"

He sounds almost angry, which catches me off guard as he glares at me. Hell, he looks positively pissed off. Of all the potential reactions I had anticipated, this was not one I had considered. Maybe nonchalant indifference. Even a smug *yeah, I knew you would call because I asked.* I had not expected angry. I am thrown and feel like running back out of the door, but that is not an option. I find I am unable to move, instead frozen to the spot by the fury in his face. Why is he angry? I conclude it must be due to the fact he did not get his own way.

"I've been busy with Mum and a wedding order at the shop." My words blurt out and trail off as I look away.

"Don't make excuses. If you didn't want to see me, that's fine," he snaps in reply.

This really is not going as planned. I am struggling to understand why it is such a big deal to him that I did not ring. I want to scream. It is pretty much all I have thought about since that night.

"No, I did. I do. It's not that. I really do. It's . . ." I lose my words again, and the whole situation begins to feel hopeless. I am back in the moment, remembering his lips on mine and his hands all over my body. I feel the heat rising in my cheeks.

His tone softens. "What? You're embarrassed about what happened?" He sounds incredulous, but at least he gets it now.

I feel a little more composed, refusing to let him see he is getting to me.

I look back at him "Yes. I'm embarrassed and remembering what you said about other girls in your club. I don't want you to think that about me."

Walking out from behind the counter, he frowns, processing what I have said. "Come here." His voice has a tone of instruction, not request.

I step forward, and he reaches his arms around, me pulling me into him. His body is soft and warm through the apron he is wearing. A current of electricity moves through me. That smell — the smell of him — woody and fresh like the ocean. I catch my breath as we pull apart, and he finds my gaze once more with his.

"Silly girl," he scolds, and I feel even sillier if possible. "Don't ever think of yourself like that or think I could think of you like that. If that were the case, I wouldn't have asked you to call me or noticed that you hadn't."

He is standing close to me. I feel the connection pulling me into him like a magnet, an invisible force I could not step away from even if I wanted to. Does he feel it, too? His expression gives nothing away to suggest he does.

"You're here later today. Are you not looking after your mum?"

We are back to making small talk and exchanging pleasantries. I am glad for the change in direction. "No. She has a gentleman friend visiting so would rather I was not around."

Ordered, would be more accurate. Kenneth has been a loyal follower for years and will have brought her a selection of sticky buns, chocolates, and flowers. My mother has him wrapped round her little finger. I am never sure what he gets in return from the relationship. He has never married, so maybe just companionship.

Gabriel smiles, the warmth radiating from his face. He has completely returned. He is back to the unknown man who has brightened my days for the last few months. "Have you eaten?"

I shake my head. Well, a packet of chocolate hobnobs with Lucy at the shop, but the less said about it the better.

"Let me cook you lunch."

"Are you not closing up?"

He half-laughs. "That's the great thing about being the boss. Just give me ten minutes to let the staff go. You can have anything off the menu as long as it's grilled chicken and Greek salad."

I find myself smiling. "Sounds lovely, but I'm intrigued. Why chicken and salad?"

"It's just about the only thing I can cook off the menu without assistance, except breakfast. I make really good breakfast." He winks at me suggestively.

"Sounds good." It genuinely does.

His smile widens.

I feel the heat in my cheeks again as I replay what I have just said. "I mean the chicken."

"I know," he replies more earnestly. "Go grab a seat. I'll

bring you a drink. Chardonnay?"

Gosh, drinking in the day. It takes me back to a time when I got to do leisurely long lunches and late suppers. I just nod. He returns in a few minutes with a large glass of wine. A young man and two women I recognise as waitresses are leaving and glance at me curiously. He seems not to notice or does not care.

"Give me about another twenty minutes or so."

He has removed the apron now, revealing a fitted grey V-neck t-shirt which clings to his frame as if he is not wearing a shirt at all. His body is lean and toned, the physique of someone who clearly works out and takes care of them self.

I nod, though it is not really a question. He disappears again as I watch him walk away. Tight washed out, blue jeans. Yes, he works out, unlike me. I feel self-conscious again and take a large swig of wine, which helps. The room fills with floaty, contemporary folk music, which reminds me of summer holidays. He has switched the music back on. I start to relax a little, watching the people outside walk up and down the street. He arrives back with two plates of chicken and salad. A bottle of wine and another glass is tucked under his arm. He looks almost flustered as he puts the food down. It occurs to me maybe he is anxious about what I will think of it. He watches as I take a bite of the chicken. It is herb scented with lemon and garlic. Delicious, as is the salad which is dressed with some sort of vinegar and mint.

"What do you think?" He fixes his eyes on mine.

"It's delicious. Where did you learn how to cook Greek food?"

He smiles, any residual tension quickly evaporating.

"My grandfather is Greek Cypriot. My mother's father. I spent quite a bit of time with him and my grandmother as a kid. Lots of big family gatherings and food."

He speaks about them with a tone of genuine affection.

"Are you from a big family?"

"Yes, I'm one of six. Two sisters and three brothers. I'm the youngest boy."

"Are you close?"

His smile drops slightly. "No, not really."

We are over halfway through the wine as he pours the remainder into our glasses. The conversation flows easily, like we are old acquaintances. We talk about my life before I moved back to look after my mother, London, and the books I was studying as part of my postgraduate degree. He is well read, and it is nice to talk to someone who seems to have similar tastes in reading and art. I discover he went to Oxford University, where he studied economics and philosophy, followed by a postgraduate degree in the States at Stanford University, where he studied business. He worked in the financial markets for a few years afterwards but got bored and wanted to create something. At twenty-nine, he has this shop and a couple of others, the club, a luxury spa resort, a golf club just outside London, an apartment for business in New York, and various other enterprises he doesn't elaborate on. He still has a modest portfolio of shares to keep his hand in and for cashflow, around two million.

I try not to choke on my wine. Despite the money, clear wealth, and quiet confidence, he is not arrogant, and there is little boast. He talks pragmatically and is down to earth, like it is the most normal thing in the world. He is engaging and charming with a hint of shyness, which makes him even more attractive. He loves to travel and to surf. He also loves art and regularly invests in pieces, especially by local Westcountry artists. I glance at my watch.

He reads my mind. "Do you need to go?"

"Yes." I nod.

He leans forward slightly. "I would really like to see you again. When would be good?"

He assumes I want to see him again, which I do. He is staring at me, like he is undressing me with his eyes. His gaze is uncompromising. I would love to know what he is actually thinking.

"Um, this weekend?" I reply.

He maintains eye contact but breaks into a smile — the one which lights up his entire face and makes his eyes dance. "Great. When, though? I assume you have to look after your mum."

I shake my head. "Not this weekend. My brother David is staying for the week, so whenever suits you. It would be good to escape."

He narrows his eyes, as he scrutinizes me. "You don't get on?"

"No." I try to keep my tone lighter than the reality. "He lives in Somerset with his wife, Verena, and their three children. This is the first time he has been back since I came home to look after Mum. We don't get on. Not at all, really." If I was being honest, I would say I am absolutely dreading it. My mother utterly adores him, and he can do no wrong unlike me.

He tilts his head to one side, biting his bottom lip. "Come and stay with me for the week."

"What?" I blurt out. I am sure I have misheard him.

He smiles calmly as I try to pick myself up off the floor. "Come stay with me. I have the room. I like your company. I want to get to know you better. No big deal."

This is not happening. No big deal? I am utterly lost for words.

It does not appear to faze him. "Come for dinner tomorrow, say around four, and if you want to stay, bring a bag. If not, no problem. I'll make sure you get home."

I cannot form any coherent thoughts, let alone formulate a sentence.

"Is that okay, Emily?" He presses for an answer.

I nod in response, still not quite believing this is happening.

He smiles, clearly amused. "Great. Write down your address, and my driver will pick you up." He pushes a serviette towards me and a pencil from behind his ear.

He has a driver, confirming my view we are from completely different worlds. My anxiety rises again. I scribble down my address, and he walks me to the door. As I reach it, he grabs my hand in his, spinning me around. The touch sears through my body like a shock of electricity. He pulls me, slamming me into him, catching me in his arms. His mouth is on mine before I can completely register what is happening. He prises my lips apart with his to deepen his kiss, giving his tongue easy access to mine. I can taste the wine as he explores my mouth. The smell of him is intoxicating. The usual sandalwood, but also amber and musk today. He runs his tongue over my bottom lip then bites it gently. I shiver, pressing my body into his, wondering if he will always have this effect on me.

He grins. "I promise it will be nice."

CHAPTER SEVEN

I get back to the house in a daze, to find Kenneth has been invited to stay for dinner. I am immediately thankful I have already made a cottage pie the night before, which I would not be wanting now anyway. I chop some broccoli and prepare my mother's medicines, only to be startled by a knock on the back door.

Lucy bursts in. "Was he there?"

"Yes." I am still processing the afternoon myself.

"Well? What happened?"

"We had lunch." I think I am in shock. I certainly cannot manage full conversation.

Lucy sighs, clearly frustrated. "Well, and?"

"He asked me to stay for the week."

Her mouth drops open. "What! Details. I need details."

Defeated, I put the kettle on and explain. After two cups of tea with a brief pause to serve dinner in the next room, I am no clearer what I am going to do.

"What are you going to do?" Lucy asks the obvious question.

I shrug. "No clue but going would seem like a really bad idea. I mean, I hardly know him."

"Sure, it's different and a bit quick, but you like him. You could always leave if you want and come back to ours. It's not as if he'd be holding you hostage."

I roll my eyes. "You're not seriously suggesting I go and stay with him?"

She smiles in response. "I don't know, Em, but it beats

staying here with your mother and David. You may regret it if you don't. I mean, what do you have to lose?"

On that point I do not have an answer. After a sleepless night, with several requests from Mother to change the TV channel and make hot chocolate, I am no clearer in the morning. Mother is sleeping in, which is her usual routine. I clean the rest of the house and make a casserole for the evening. The rest of my day hurtles past me in a blur. Mother takes most of my time when she wakes, fussing about David's imminent arrival. She insists on changing her outfit three times and her nail colour twice. David is ten years older than me, a bully of the worst kind, and always has been. My mother dotes on him and regularly reminds me that when she discovered she was pregnant with me, she thought she was starting the early menopause.

He strides in at three in the afternoon, ignoring me and kissing her on both cheeks. "Hello, Mother. You look so well."

She laps it up, instructing me to make a pot of tea and dismissing me with a flick of her hand.

David follows me to the kitchen. "You've put on weight since I last saw you."

If anything, I have lost some. I turn to look at him. I may not exactly be supermodel material, but you could probably fit two of me into his trousers. I decide it is best not to rise to the bait, based on past experience.

He smirks as he continues. "Anyway. I want to spend time with Mother, so I will need you to do all the day-to-day stuff. Medicines. Meals. Mother's daily care. Housework. Anything I need. I am here to focus on Mother and keep her company."

This is about right. Mother has been gushing to anyone who will listen about how her beloved son has taken a week off from his very important job to look after her properly.

"No." The words escape my lips before my brain fully engages.

He narrows his eyes, squinting at me suspiciously. "What do you mean, no?"

"No, it's not okay, David, or possible, I'm afraid. I'm going away for a few days. I wanted to give you and Mother some space."

He glares at me. I have no idea where my sudden bravery has come from.

"Cancel it." His tone is indignant and angry now.

I shake my head. "No, sorry, I can't. I've made dinner for tonight, and the carers come in four times a day. There are instructions everywhere, and Mother will tell you exactly what she needs."

"Where do you really need to be? Your friends will have a much better time without you."

"Friend." I correct him.

"What friend?" He presses further.

"No one you know, and to be honest, it's none of your business."

He laughs coldly. "A man? So you've finally found one stupid enough to be interested in you. Does he know what he's let himself in for? Look at you, you frigid frump. Does Mother know? Cancel before I tell her."

His words sting, and he will tell her anyway. I shake my head and walk past him. He starts shouting something about my duties and responsibilities. He is clearly in shock, but I do not listen. I am shocked myself in that I have finally stood up to him. Shocked also that I have finally made a decision, although probably the least sensible option, after dithering all day. I suddenly feel free.

CHAPTER EIGHT

Painfully aware of the time, I have the quickest shower in history. I am thankful I shaved my legs yesterday and washed my hair. What am I doing? What am I actually doing? Sure, I do not want to be here, but I have no idea where I am going. Frying pans and fires spring to mind. With no time to really think, I pull on a pair of jeans and a green blouse. I put on the strappy sandals I wore to his club, pull my hair into a high ponytail, and apply some lip gloss. I throw together some clothes into a bag, mindful of the changeable May weather but unsure what to pack or what we will be doing, or if we will even be doing anything together at all. I pack some toiletries and include the least frumpy and functional underwear I own, which does not leave too many options. I glance at the clock. It is five minutes until four. No time to dwell further. I toss my kindle into the bag, throw on my mac, and grab my handbag.

Mother is waiting for me with David. He has clearly told her.

"Who is he?" She scrutinises me with beady eyes. Her tone is cold and nasty.

"Just a friend," I reply hastily.

"Humph. Heterosexual men don't have female friends. You're either lying, or he's gay. Which is it?"

I kiss her cheek and try to avoid eye contact. "It's neither, Mum. He's just a friend."

She tuts. "Are you really going to leave an old, defenceless woman to fend for herself?"

34

I frown. "No, Mum, of course not. David is here, and he has come to look after you."

She glares at me, as does he. "Unbelievable. So you're piling all the responsibility onto your brother who works so hard. Run along, then."

I want to scream. It is so unfair. I know my brother will leave with a sizeable cheque from my mother's savings. I never ask or want anything, and I have given up everything to care for her. This is the first time she has seen him for nine months, even though he lives closer than I did. They both glower at me. I know there is little point saying anything further. I turn and leave like a scolded dog with its tail between its legs.

The heat hits me as I open the front door. It is far hotter than it looked from the window, and it occurs to me I have not been outside today. I see the car straight away, a black Audi with dark windows. At least, I think it is an Audi. A formally dressed older man stands beside it. Knowing David will be watching from the window, I do not look back.

The man smiles warmly when he sees me. He reminds me of the police in the way he holds himself and his stance.

"Miss Black?" His tone is formal but kind somehow.

I nod, and he takes my bag whilst opening the car door for me. This is different. I feel like I am some sort of celebrity and more than a little ridiculous. I wonder why I could not have just got a taxi or met him at the shop or club.

"Ready to go, Miss Black?"

I have literally no idea where I am actually going. "Yes, thank you. Please, could you let me have Mr. Hunter-Law's address?"

I see him frown slightly in the rear-view mirror.

"Yes, of course. It's Bay View, Old Salcombe Road."

I smile. "Thank you."

He smiles in response, returning the gesture. "No problem. We should be there in about forty minutes, depending on the traffic."

I text the address to Lucy, adding, *In case he's an axe murderer*

Her response is almost instant. *OMG you actually went!?!*

Yep, mad or stupid or both!

Have fun, hun, take care, and keep in touch xx

Forty minutes later we pull off the main road along a much narrower C road. It winds along the coastline, revealing glimpses of the sea behind the tall Devon hedges. We pass very few houses and a lonely pub called *The Winkle Inn*. Eventually we stop in front of a large white house, standing alone and proud over an undisturbed panoramic view of the coastline. It's sleek and modern looking, spanning two floors, from what I can see. A line of four large picture windows shimmer in the late afternoon sun.

"Wow." I do not mean to speak out loud, but the words articulate anyway.

I see the driver half-smile in the mirror. "Yes, it is impressive. He rarely brings people up here."

I wonder why the driver has told me this, but do not have time to think on it further. He opens the car door, and I am escorted, with my bag, to the front door.

CHAPTER NINE

He answers the door in blue jeans and a white linen shirt. The top buttons of his shirt are undone, which reveal his chest and a glimpse of a light splattering of hair. He's barefoot. Even his feet are beautiful.

He smiles as the driver drops my bag on the floor beside me. "Thank you, Guy."

The driver nods and is gone, leaving us alone. The enormity of what I am doing hits me like a tidal wave. Here I am with a man I barely know-in a remote house—in the middle of nowhere. What on earth am I doing? We stand awkwardly in the entrance hall for a moment. I feel like my feet have taken root.

He senses my unease, asking, "You okay?"

I nod weakly.

He looks unconvinced but chooses not to pursue it further. "Come get a drink. I will show you around."

I follow him down a few steps into a huge open-plan room with entrances leading to hallways off to each side. Opposite us the far wall is a floor to ceiling window, with a spectacular view of the sea and the horizon. The sun cascades into the room with such intensity it almost glows. All the other walls are pure white. There is a state-of-the-art kitchen on the right-hand side with black granite worksurfaces. The main area has a collection of leather sofas and a long wooden coffee table with a large glass bowl in turquoise which catches the sunlight bouncing all around us.

I stand beside an island in the kitchen while he pulls a

bottle of wine from the fridge and pours two glasses. The tension sizzles between us, and I feel slightly nauseous. I reach for my wine, and my hands develop a life of their own. The glass crashes down against the counter away from me, spilling its contents everywhere, including over his shirt. By some miracle, the glass does not break.

"I'm so sorry." Immediately I look around me for something to wipe up the liquid, to no avail. I feel awful, embarrassed, clumsy, and exposed. I do everything I can to avoid eye contact, though I can feel him looking at me.

"It's fine." His voice is calm and soothing. "No harm done."

I take a chance and glance up to see him removing his wet shirt, which he proceeds to use to mop up the wine before pouring me another glass. He moves to the other side of the island to stand in front of me. He is close enough to smell sandalwood and limes. His chest and stomach are well toned and muscular, as I would have expected. His skin is tanned and smooth. The splattering of hair on his chest continues in a thin trail under his belly button into his jeans, which hang low on his hips. He looks like the men you see in magazines and films. I try not to stare, but I know I am gawping at him, and he is fully aware of the fact. My eyes meet his to find his expression vaguely amused. There are no words, but the silence speaks volumes. He is breathtakingly beautiful, and I am painfully aware I am well out of my depth. I look away, back out to sea, breaking the connection between us.

After what feels like a long period of time, he finally speaks. "I am going to speak really plainly, which may shock you, but I don't want you to be feeling anxious the whole time you're here." He pauses, letting the words sink in as he finds my eyes with his once more. His voice is husky and deep. "Emily, I want to fuck you in every way imaginable. I've wanted to fuck you for a long time, and in this last week, pretty much any coherent thoughts I have had, awake or asleep, have been about being inside you." He pauses once more, holding me in place with his eyes. His stare is authoritative and firm.

My anxiety creeps up a notch. As much as I think I want it, too, I am sure I will be an utter disappointment to him. I don't need to look to know my eyes are wide. I must look like a rabbit caught in the headlights. I take a large gulp of wine. I do not taste it, and it burns my throat.

He smiles softly and continues. "I think it's what you want, too, but for whatever reason, the thought of me fucking you makes you nervous. The thing is, as much as I want it, that's not why I asked you here. It was an impulsive thing. I meant it when I said I like your company. I'd like to get to know you better, which is a new one on me, but I find you interesting. Yeah, I would like to have sex with you. I would like that very much, but it's not why I asked you here, and I certainly don't expect it. If it happens, great. If it doesn't, it's no problem. We can just be friends, and that's what it's meant to be. Maybe that's the connection I've been feeling with you. Either way, it will be your choice, when and if you decide to go there with me. Does that help?"

I let the words sink in. He is right. It is the elephant in the room, which is now dancing around in a tutu with glitter paint making a complete spectacle of itself. I do relax, though. I am still shocked by his frankness but thankful for it at the same time. I nod, taking another gulp of wine. I taste it this time. It is fruity and dry.

He smiles once more, seeming pleased I have relaxed a little. "Great. Let's change things around. I'm going to go for a run. I'll show you to your room, and you can relax. Have a bath, or read, or whatever. Then we can start again. Sound good?"

His words sound less of a question and more of a request

but still like a good idea. I nod once more, and he retrieves my bag from the entrance, walking me down a long hallway to the left. The same flooring and whitewashed walls run all through the entire floor. At the end of the hall is a spacious, airy room with a picture window. It overlooks the sea, like most of the windows. A large white metal framed bed sits to one side with blue striped covers. There is a large white wardrobe, vanity table, and chair. Other than this, the room is empty, except for a single door which I can only guess is a bathroom.

"This is your room." He puts my bag on the bed. "And bathroom."

He pushes the door open to reveal a bathroom with a large white bathtub and the same outlook over the sea. There is an array of expensive looking toiletries on the shelf, along with a pile of fluffy towels and a bathrobe on a distressed wooden chair.

"Help yourself to whatever. I asked my housekeeper to make sure you have everything you might need."

Housekeeper? Of course, he has a housekeeper.

"This is wonderful. Thank you." It is. Like staying in a luxury hotel. "Where is your room?" I am not sure why I am asking him this question.

He does not show any reaction. "Down the other hallway. I'll leave you to get settled in."

He is gone, and I feel instantly calmed. Maybe it is the sound of the sea crashing on the rocks below. I run a long bath with bath oil from the shelf while I unpack, which does not take long. The bath is divine, covering my body with an oily sheen and the scent of rose and ylang-ylang. I cannot remember the last time I took a long uninterrupted bath. The water is soothing and washes away my misgivings.

I dress back into my jeans and a light blouse more suitable to the warm weather. The floor is warm with underfloor heating, so I leave my shoes off. I am glad now I let Lucy paint my toenails cherry red a few days ago. I glance at my watch. It has been an hour, so I assume he will be back soon.

Back in the kitchen, I finish my wine and inquisitively walk down the other hallway into his bedroom. It is another vast space. Again, a floor to ceiling window, but also glass doors opening out to what looks like a balcony under the eaves of the roof. The room smells of him. The bed is huge, with a dark wood headboard and bedside cabinets to match. Like my room, there is another door, but this one leads into a walk-in wardrobe with the same dark wood. The only things visible, are a line of slick tailored suits and formal jackets. To the other side is a bathroom. Again, very little is on display except a bottle of cologne and some shower gel on the shelf.

As I walk back to the kitchen, I stop dead to find him there in running tracks and a black t-shirt which clings to him. His hair is damp with sweat, which makes him look even hotter. I flush with embarrassment, having been caught snooping.

"Nice bath?" He looks amused but says nothing more.

I nod, lost for words, feeling the heat rising up my neck into my cheeks.

He brushes past me. "Good. I'm going to grab a quick shower."

CHAPTER TEN

He emerges a little later in black jeans and a black shirt. He pours us some more wine, and I follow him down a long spiral staircase to the floor below. The décor is similar to the floor above, but the back wall, where the front door would be, is floor to ceiling with books. There are hallways to each side like upstairs. He explains the one to the left leads to his study. We go straight ahead through a set of French doors onto a large balcony overlooking the spectacular sea view and rocks below. It has low glass walls, what looks to be a hot tub, and a glass table with black metal chairs. We sit for some time in the late evening sun, drinking wine and eating olives with antipasti and cheese. As before, the conversation flows easily, and the tension leaves me.

"More wine?" he asks.

I should have kept a better tab of how much I have been drinking, starting to feel a little tipsy. "Are you trying to get me drunk?" The alcohol has also relaxed my tongue.

He smiles mischievously. "Maybe. Come here. You feel miles away." He gestures to the sofa next to him, and I move a little unsteadily. He puts his arm around me, still smiling. "You're so pretty."

I blush, and he tucks a piece of stray hair behind my ear, which makes me shiver. Kissing me long and slow, he sucks and flickers his tongue around mine leisurely. I hear a boat horn, and he stops. We both look over the balcony to see a yacht with two men and three women, all waving.

"Hey, Gabe. What you up to?" one of the men shouts up.

He says nothing and just waves back as they pass.

"Are they your friends?" It's an innocent enough question. He frowns slightly. "No, just people I know."

The sun is setting and melting into the sky, in a blaze of ochre and red. We watch it disappear into darkness, listening to the waves gently lapping on the rocks below us. He slides his arm back around me. I am glad to be close to him again. The sea breeze is more chilled now as the night air lingers. We kiss once more with the same lazy intensity. He circles his other arm around my waist, pulling me into him.

I want him. I really want him. The smell of him fills my senses, and my inhibitions are fading. I don't know if it is the wine or the location, or the freedom, but everything in me aches for him and is all consumed by him in this moment. The sun completely disappears into blackness. Tall columns of light illuminate around us. I can hear crickets in the cliff grass.

"We should move inside." His voice is even huskier now. "What would you like to do?"

I pause, and he smiles. I smile back, and he looks slightly confused.

"I'd like you to take me to bed, Gabriel." The wine has definitely increased my confidence.

He looks momentarily taken aback. Reaching for my hand, he leads me up the stairs to his bedroom. We stand a little way from the foot of his bed. The lighting is soft, and I can still hear the faint sound of the sea. It should be relaxing, but I am far from relaxed. The enormity of what I am about to do threatens to overwhelm me.

He stands in front of me, surveying and undressing me with his eyes like l am something to eat. "You must tell me if I do something you don't like or you want me to stop." His voice is quietly hushed.

I can barely begin to imagine what he is going to do to me. Before I can think further, he presses his lips to mine once more and kisses me hard. He moves his tongue deep in my mouth. Gone is the leisurely laziness. He places one of his hands around my waist, resting the other at the back of my neck, stroking my skin with the tips of his fingers. I hang like a ragdoll in his arms, savouring his closeness and his touch. Pulling back, he unbuttons my blouse slowly, deliberately slow, while he watches me with an uncompromising stare, his lips slightly ajar. He lowers his gaze and brushes his hand over the bare skin on my stomach and waist so softly it almost tickles. It makes my breathing race.

He finds me again with his eyes. "You're so beautiful."

I feel myself frown.

His eyes continue to lock on mine. "You don't agree?"

I shake my head. "I know I need to lose some weight."

He smiles. "No, you don't. You're voluptuous and curvy. I like that. I like your softness, something to hold onto. Most men do."

I don't believe him. The images of him from the tabloids with stick-thin models and actresses flood into my brain. Before I have time to argue, he drops to his knees and kisses my stomach. He moves up to my neck, leaving a scorching trail of kisses across my breasts and along my shoulders. His stubble gently grazes my skin as he massages my breasts through the lace of my bra. He circles his fingers around my nipples, which grow firm beneath his caress. Reaching up, he pushes the blouse off my shoulders, unhooking my bra. My breasts bounce free.

Smiling once more while he takes in the view, he removes his shirt over his head. His eyes are carnal and dark — he looks like he is about to devour me. He kisses me again with a hunger. I anticipate it this time and reciprocate. Stroking his hands down the length of my bare back, he pulls me against him until the hair on his chest tickles my nipples. I reach my arms around him. His skin is smooth. The muscles on his arms and back are hard beneath my fingers. I feel his teeth against my skin as he moves his mouth down my neck and chest until my nipple is in his mouth. I gasp at the soft, warm wetness of his tongue as he flickers over it. Moving across to the other nipple, he replaces his mouth with his fingers, less gentle now. My nipples are swollen and hard under his touch, a direct line to everything between my legs. I feel myself wet and wanting. I am back in the club, but this time I do not think I am capable of holding back even if I wanted to.

"You okay?" He murmurs, finding my eyes with his.

I nod, and he kisses my stomach once more while undoing my jeans, moving his hands down under the denim into my knickers. Cupping my buttocks, he kneads my flesh and continues to kiss me. All I can think about is him. He pushes my jeans down to my ankles, dropping to his knees as he does. I step out of them, and he nuzzles his face into my crotch, kissing me through the cotton fabric of my knickers. Standing, he pulls me onto the bed, with him lying half on top of me. The sheets are cold beneath us. He rests his knee between my legs, and I feel his growing erection through his jeans against my thigh. He is so close. The smell of sandalwood and musk from his cologne is all around me. We kiss again with urgency. He glides his hands over my almost naked body, every nerve ending sensitised and alive. Stroking, kneading, and exploring, he moves his hand gently along my inner thigh and over my knickers.

I am wet between my legs, which almost embarrasses me. I want him badly, and he must know it. My nipples stand tall like flagpoles, so alert they are almost painful. Moving his fingers under the fabric, he strokes gently over my clitoris, while he continues to explore my mouth with his tongue. I move my hips up instinctively to meet his touch. He strokes gently with his fingers. Then harder, circling and teasing. The palm of his hand covers my pubic hair as he enters me with a finger. His finger circles inside me, massaging my innermost walls, whilst his thumb firmly rubs my clitoris. He pulls back to look into my eyes.

"You're so wet," he whispers.

"Is that bad?" I can barely string a sentence together. The tension is building between my legs to a point I might internally combust. I have never felt this or wanted anyone in the way I want him.

He smiles. "No, sweet Emily, that is a good thing for both of us."

He continues to move his fingers inside me. Two now, circling in and out, while he teases my nipples with his lips once more. Lightheaded, I find my hips have moved up to meet his hand, and my whole-body aches for him.

Abruptly he stops, gently removing his fingers. "Shit!"

I am immediately transported back to the scene of my doomed sympathy sex. He leans over to the drawer next to the bed, the bulge in his trousers against my hip. I wonder what the issue is.

He hangs his head, shaking it slowly, looking away from me. "Sorry, babe."

Completely exposed and awkward, I lie there desperately missing his touch, equally embarrassed and trying to work out what has gone wrong. He sits up, and I see the unmistakeable bulge in his trousers. His erection is straining in his jeans.

His eyes find mine again now. He is still looking at me like I am something to eat, but he's also blushing slightly. "I'm sorry. I don't have any condoms. I do at work, but I don't bring people back here usually." He brushes his hand through his hair hurriedly. "Fuck. I feel like a teenager. Piss poor planning, but I guess I really didn't think this would happen tonight."

"I'm on the pill." The words blurt out.

He frowns, looking uncertain.

I explain. "Hormones and stuff, but it also means I won't get pregnant."

He shakes his head a little. "It's not just that."

I understand what he means, blushing myself before clarifying. "Right. Well, I've not been with anyone for over a year, and only ever with two people. Well, one and a half, and never without protection. I don't have anything, and I guess you would know."

He smiles cautiously. "Yeah, I get tested regularly and was completely clean at my check a few months ago. Maybe unbelievably, though true, I haven't fucked anyone since then."

"We're good, then." I cannot believe what I am saying. My inhibition and caution have left me writhing desperately underneath his gorgeous man. Maybe it is not the most sensible thing, but I do not really care in this moment. I am sick of always making and being expected to make the sensible choices.

There is a moment of silence between us, and he is still frowning. "Are you sure? It's not something I would ever normally do. Which I know probably sounds like a line, but again, it's true."

I stroke his bare back. "Nor me, Gabriel."

He raises an eyebrow. The irony is not lost on either of us.

"Please. I really want this. I really want you." Too honest, but it is the truth.

Smiling gently, he kisses me slowly at first but then more urgently before he stands and glides my knickers down over my legs. He removes his own jeans and boxer shorts. Oh my. He stands naked in front of me, and he is truly gorgeous. His legs are toned, tanned, and muscular like the rest of him, with the same soft dark hair as his chest, but that is not where I find my eyes focusing. His penis is fully erect, long, and smooth. His pubic hair is dark and thick. He looks huge, and I wonder how he will feel inside me, if he will even fit inside me. He is looking at me with the same hunger as before.

"Are you sure you want to do this?" His voice is low and seductive.

I nod, and he climbs back onto the bed, kissing me. We fall back into the position we were in before. He runs his hands over my body once more, finding my nipples and tweaking them to attention to the point that I am panting. My legs are fully open, and I wrap them loosely around him.

"You are so beautiful." His eyes are warm like liquid mahogany. He slides his hand back down between my thighs. "And so wet."

He smiles in apparent approval. His fingers enter me once more. His thumb rubs against my clitoris, more roughly now. I'm so sensitive, I think I might lose it. I am not sure I can stand it much longer.

"Are you ready, Emily?" It is a rhetorical question, but I nod anyway.

He moves up until he is fully lying on top of me, his weight supported by his arms. I feel nervous, but all I want is to feel him inside of me. He pushes his penis gently between my legs. Pulling my thighs up around him, he moves his hands to my lower back and tilts my hips towards him. My breathing hitches slightly as he kisses my neck. He pulls back, looking into my eyes as he enters me slowly. My vagina stretches around the head of his penis as he pushes his length inside me. It feels unfamiliar and uncomfortable. So full.

His eyes do not leave mine. His voice is almost a whisper now. "Are you okay? You're so tight."

I nod, and he moves slowly as I get used to him inside me, my body stretching to accommodate him. I feel the moisture between my legs as he circles his hips. He moves in and out of me, pushing deeper, making me shudder. He strokes his hands over my body, and I stretch my legs further around him. I grip his back with my hands. A smile flickers across his face, knowing and sensual, and he kisses me with the same slow rhythm as his circling hips. It no longer feels uncomfortable. Instead it feels full and needed as we move against one another, and I relax into him. I reach my hands down to his buttocks, taut and firm, pulling him further into me. Our bodies press together. I raise my legs higher around him, and he thrusts deeper and deeper inside me.

The sound of our breathing is accelerated and ragged. We glide and grind our bodies against one another like they have moulded into one. He rests his head on my shoulder. His breath is warm on my skin. I bring my legs together around him. My clitoris quivers and aches. I rub myself against his pubic bone, desperate for the friction as it builds. The warmth and sensation spread out through my whole body. At the edge of the cliff, I go over it. I am entirely undone as the throbbing grows and builds in intensity until my whole body is a jumble of pulsating, sensitised nerve endings. I explode. I am his completely. His name is on my lips as I writhe and groan beneath him. Then, he fills me as he comes.

CHAPTER ELEVEN

I wake up feeling a little disorientated. Daylight floods into the room, and I am in Gabriel's bed. It feels early. As my eyes become accustomed to the light, I see he is in bed beside me. He is sitting on top of the covers. His legs are outstretched in black cotton pyjama trousers, and he is bare-chested as he types on a laptop. He is also wearing glasses, which I have not seen him do before. It makes him look even sexier.

He smiles when he sees I'm awake. "Good morning, Emily. How are you today?"

I miss the meaning in his words, just smiling back like an inane fool. I thought I would feel awkward the next morning, but I'm not. Instead I'm happy and completely naked next to the man I have just given myself to. He looks gorgeous and fresh. I imagine I have severe bed hair.

He seems vaguely amused as he continues. "There is some juice on the table beside you."

I turn to look at the bedside table and see a glass of freshly squeezed orange juice, which I drink eagerly.

"Are you hungry?" he enquires.

I nod, turning back to him.

He smiles, still looking amused. "What would you like?"

Oh, good grief. He even sounds seductive when offering to make me breakfast. I sit up, pulling the covers around me. I know what I want. I lean towards him and take off his glasses. Frowning a little, he seems confused. I push my lips to his. He responds immediately as I run my tongue over his bottom lip. I can taste coffee and smell fresh limes, realising his hair is still damp from the shower.

Raising an eyebrow, he grins and puts his laptop on the table next to him. "I asked what you wanted for breakfast."

"I know. That was my answer." I feel confident and empowered suddenly.

He laughs. "At least you didn't make any references to sausages. It's become a really old joke at the shop."

"We wouldn't want to bore, sir," I tease, feeling bold and flirtatious.

He narrows his eyes. "I would be very careful calling me sir."

Without warning he pulls the sheet away to reveal me in all my nakedness. He runs his eyes shamelessly over my body, over every curve and imperfection. His lips are slightly ajar. I feel very on show and uncomfortable despite my earlier rush of confidence, unused to the attention.

He senses it, tilting my face upwards so our eyes meet. "You're beautiful, Emily. Please, don't ever forget that." His voice is deep and earnest.

My body wakes up in response when he kisses me again and pushes me back onto the bed with him. Moving with him in the moment, I relax.

"Roll over onto your side." His tone is commanding.

I do what he asks, full of nervous excitement but less on display. He runs his nails down my back and bottom slowly. I arch my back with wanton expectation. Putting his arms around me, he pulls me back against him. His growing erection teases at the small of my back. He pulls my hair away from my neck, grazing my skin with his teeth and circling his nails over my breasts and stomach. I push my naked bottom back into his crotch. Cupping my breasts in his hands, he rolls my nipples between his thumb and forefingers until they are pert and erect, his touch less gentle than the night before. My body wakes up and responds to him as his erection grows stronger against my buttocks. He moves his hands between my legs, circling my clitoris. With one hand he pulls my pubic hair upwards, while his other hand gains easy access to my labia. He dips his fingers in and out of me, coating them in the growing wetness there.

"You're eager this morning." His voice is deep. There is more than a hint of darkness and danger in it. "Kneel up for me."

Again, an instruction rather than a request. Does it bother me? No. I am caught up in the moment. Happy to go with it and enjoying this game, I do as he asks. The awkwardness in me is present, but not dominant. I am completely turned on and wanting more.

"Lean forward for me so you're holding the headboard." His voice is unexpectantly cool.

I cannot see him, which heightens the anticipation and excitement. Once more I do as he asks. I outstretch my arms so my hands grasp the wood. My thighs are straight, and my bottom is in the air.

"Move your legs apart," he orders.

I comply, willingly.

"Further," he demands.

The anticipation makes me even wetter. I am aware he can see everything, which puts me on display, almost vulnerable, but also utterly turned on. Excited as I wait for what is coming next, my breasts swing below me like pendulums.

"Quite the view." His voice is husky again, and I hear the lust in it.

I still cannot see him, but I feel him as he runs his nails down across my buttocks and thighs. I shudder, wanting his touch as he repeats the action slowly. I arch my back like a cat and feel him move closer to me. He pushes his fingers inside me. I gasp a little. The sensation is deep and full.

"Move for me, babe," he commands, moving his thumb up

to massage my clitoris.

I roll my hips. I am fully aware he is watching me from behind. Waves of sensation move through my body as he continues to rub and tease between my legs. I am close, so close. Every time I nearly reach my climax, he slows a little, deliberately prolonging the wait. I am wound tight like a spring. My breathing is ragged. I cannot bear it much longer.

"Please, Gabriel." My voice escapes me in desperation. I need him. I want him and the release.

Resting his other hand on my bottom to still me, he removes his fingers. I know it is imminent now, but he makes me wait. All I can hear is my breathing in a pant. My vagina feels empty and wet where he has left me. He moves behind me and places his hands on my hips, thrusting into me with a single motion. I groan as he fills and stretches me. He feels even bigger in this position, as if he should not fit. I stretch around him anyway, greedy to take everything he has. I lean back into him. It forces him deeper inside of me, his thighs flat against mine. Responding accordingly, he grasps my hips firmly in his hands, pulling me back to him as he thrusts mercilessly. Everything in me clenches, quickly followed by the release, like a wave of ecstasy moving through me until even my fingertips tingle.

Pulling me up so I am almost sitting in his lap, he slows as I continue to move on him. He finds my nipples with his fingers once more, almost pinching as he fondles them. It sends a surge of electricity down my body to between my legs. Then he moves down to find my clitoris, swollen from all the attention. I am close again as he continues to thrust into me, riding on throbbing waves of warmth. His penis is still hard as stone inside me. I know he is far from done, although my own movements are minimal.

He continues to tease my nipples and clitoris, but more gently and slowly as the feeling builds again. We are barely moving, but he is still fully inside me, filling me with no compromise. He kisses my neck. I sigh with pleasure as he reaches my arms out in front of me and eases me forward so I am on all fours. With one hand on my stomach and the other on my lower back, he tilts my hips so my bottom moves upwards, thrusting him even deeper inside me.

The sweat on his body mixes with mine and the smell of musk and salt. Rolling his own hips, he moves his hands back onto my hips, controlling my movements so he can penetrate me fully. He thrusts relentlessly at a pace I cannot possibly keep up with. My vagina throbs and aches, tensing around him. I can barely stand it any longer. My body quivers, and I peak. Wave after wave of pleasure consumes me as he calls out my name, and we are both undone. He lowers me onto the bed, rolling over onto his back. The waves of sensation are still moving through my body. I glance across at him and am surprised to see he looks flushed. His breathing is rapid, like my own.

He finds his eyes with mine. "Fuck, Emily. What are you trying to do to me?" He looks back at the ceiling. "Are you okay? I was a little rough with you"

I cannot think of anything coherent to say. "I'm fine. More than fine. I want try new things."

He smiles darkly, rubbing his hand over his mouth. "New things? Are you experimenting with me for your new things?"

I blush, very aware he is far more experienced than me. "Yes, new things. Is it always like that?"

I can see what all the fuss is about now. Surely it cannot always be like this and mind-blowingly consuming. My own experience has never been this. Straight missionary position, generally after alcohol with the lights off or on low. If it was always this good, no one would ever get out of bed.

He frowns slightly amused, I think. "What, sex? You've

had sex before though?"

I nod. "Yes, but not like this."

Laughing, he narrows his eyes. "No, it's not always like this. Sometimes it's a bit crap or purely functional. Sometimes, it's just *nice*." He emphasises the last word. "Why are you enjoying it so far? I would never have guessed you are having a good time."

I roll my eyes. "Guess it just must be sex with you, then. I've never really been bothered before. I'm struggling to believe you ever have crap or just functional sex. Even your first time."

His frown deepens. "Let's not even go there."

A silence creeps in between us, and I feel the distance as he pulls back. I wonder what the story is, instantly regretting my comment.

He sits up without warning. "I'm going to grab a shower. I'll make us some breakfast. I'm guessing you're actually hungry for food now."

I nod. He is right. I am famished. He stands in all his naked glory. I try not to stare, which is harder said than done as he walks leisurely to the bathroom. He leaves me lying on his bed watching the sun fully rise over the sea cliffs and thinking about the events of the last twelve hours.

CHAPTER TWELVE

He reappears a little later in a pair of faded blue jeans and a check shirt. "Do you have any plans today?"

I shake my head. I had not even thought about the day yet.

"Ok, great. Do you want to join my plans?"

I nod, eagerly. I am keen to spend as much time as possible with him and find out more about him, about what makes him tick.

He raises an eyebrow. "Are you not going to even ask what those plans are before you so readily agree?"

Oh no. What have I just got myself into? "Should I be scared?" I ask with slight trepidation.

He laughs. "Maybe, but not on this occasion. I'm driving down to St Ives to pick up some art I've commissioned for the club. We could grab some lunch, and you can help me pick out some other pieces."

"Sounds good." I sound relieved, but the prospect of spending the day with him does sound good. Really good.

"I've run you a bath and will go make us some breakfast. Come find me when you're done. No rush."

I do not move. I am acutely aware that I am still completely naked under the sheet and regretting I did not at least pull on a t-shirt while he was away.

"Go on, then," he urges and smiles wickedly, completely aware of what he is doing.

Sliding out from the bed naked, I decide I do not really care. There are no clothes in the vicinity anyway to protect my modesty. Besides, he has already seen everything. He tilts his head to the side, clearly enjoying the view. I try to walk sexily past him, fully aware I am failing miserably. I attempt to suck in my belly, while my boobs sway inelegantly. All the while I try not to dwell on the fact that I suspect I look a little like a waddling duck. He slaps my backside as I walk past. It makes me yelp out from the shock more than anything.

"Miss you, sexy," he murmurs.

I can still feel him watching me, following me with his eyes, as I disappear from view.

The bath steams with clouds of lavender and jasmine. It stings a little as I sit down, but it quickly passes as I sink into the scented water. A little while later, I get dressed into a blue skirt with a daisy pattern and a light blue V-neck sweater. I have no idea what to wear, but this is flattering and accentuates the curves he has said he likes. It also shows enough cleavage to be sexy and a little cheeky without being too revealing. I look at myself in the mirror. My cheeks are flushed pink, and I look rested and fresh. No need for blusher or too much effort today to hide the paleness or the shadows under my eyes. Instead I just apply a little mascara and lip-gloss, leaving my hair loose, to cascade freely down my back. As I walk into the kitchen, I smell bacon and baking. Gabriel has his back to me and does not hear me enter. He is humming and singing along to Bon Jovi's *Livin' on a Prayer*.

It makes me smile. "I wouldn't have had you down for an eighties rock fan."

He turns abruptly. He is blushing slightly but with a huge grin, which lights up his whole face, a face which could stop traffic.

"It's the radio." He turns the music down. "You look great. I really like your hair down."

I'm off balance again. My inner feminist scolds me over how he can have such a dramatic effect on me with just a few words. I sit down on a chair by the kitchen island, and he moves towards me, placing a mug of aromatic and rich coffee in front of me. He stands close next to me, close enough to make my body ache for him. It makes me fully aware of his presence, as if I needed reminding.

"Are you sore?" The directness of his question surprises me as he focuses his eyes on mine.

"A little," I admit

"Promise, just a little?" His tone is suddenly serious.

I nod feeling more than a little embarrassed.

He smiles leaning closer to me, whispering in my ear, although it is only the two of us. "Good on two counts. One it means I will be able to seduce you again later. Second, you will remember all day what we have done together and how it feels to have me inside you."

I do not respond, feeling my cheeks burn as he returns to preparing breakfast. We eat French toast with crispy bacon and maple syrup while we watch the waves roll into the cliffs below. It is easy. The silence between us is comfortable as if we have known each other a long time.

He stands suddenly and turns the radio up. "I love this song. An ex-friend told me it summed me up." He pauses, lost in his thoughts but still grinning. "Maybe I shouldn't admit to that."

The song is *Carnation* by The Jam. He seems immersed in it as he drums his fingers on the counter to the beat.

"Was the friend female by any chance? "I ask as the song ends.

He smiles crookedly, as he laughs. "How did you guess?"

I shrug. "Call it female intuition. Thank you for breakfast. It was delicious."

"Good. We'll get going in a minute."

I watch him walk out of the kitchen. He re-emerges from his room wearing heavy, black boots and a black leather jacket which looks worn and vintage. He looks like an utter bad boy from the wrong side of town. I had not noticed the cars yesterday, a sleek black Audi R8 and a Range Rover. We take the Range Rover, which he explains means we can bring the paintings back in it. The drive to St Ives is fast. He drives with only one hand on the steering wheel, which is a little disconcerting. I also discover Gabriel does seem to have a genuine fondness for Eighties rock and Nineties Indie music. That is the radio station we listen to. He sings along without inhibition. I find myself doing the same. His mood is infectious when he is like this. A million miles away from the more serious, brooding side of him I have only seen glimpses of to date.

Lush green fields with glimpses of the ocean and picturesque Cornish villages roll past. Eventually we pull up outside a large whitewashed building on the outskirts of St Ives, perched high on the clifftops. He opens my door and takes my hand, leading me inside. His palm is warm and his grip strong. The space is enormous, airy and light, with nothing except paintings on the walls as far as the eye can see. The pictures are mainly seascapes and landscapes.

"Gabriel!" The woman behind the counter jumps up.

He smiles a genuine smile, almost shy. She is older, maybe late fifties. Her long dark hair is flecked with grey. She wears a baggy long-sleeved dress in a heavy purple fabric, with a string of blue beads and a black scarf. Her eyes are striking green, like a cat. The smell of patchouli floats around us as she moves closer, kissing him on the cheek.

"This is Emily." His hand is still firmly holding mine which she seems to note as her focus turns to me, still smiling.

"Very nice to meet you, Emily. I'm Judith."

"Nice to meet you." I respond honestly, intrigued by her. There must be something in her aura.

She smiles again, turning her attention back to Gabriel and resting her hand on his arm. "It has been too long, Gabriel.

Are you still painting?" Her tone almost scolds, and I wonder what their relationship is.

He shakes his head. "No, too busy these days. Are the commissions ready? I can take them today if they are." He blatantly dodges the question.

She smiles, seeming fully aware he has. "Of course. Completely finished and dry since you saw them with Liam a few weeks ago. I will arrange for them to be wrapped, and then you are good to go, my dear," she explains, pausing as she looks back at me. "Gabriel is a very talented artist. One of my best students. Such a shame he did not take it further."

I glance at Gabriel in surprise. I do not know why. I can see him painting now she has said it, but it seems a long way from his current enterprises.

The colour rushes to his cheeks briefly, but he quickly composes himself. "We're going to grab some lunch, but I also want to look at some other pieces while we are here." He ignores Judith's comments.

It does not phase her. "Of course. Leave me your keys, I will have Liam pack up for you."

The shop bell rings, and more people enter the gallery.

Judith raises her hand to wave at the new visitors, as she starts to move in their direction. "Come find me when you're done, Gabriel."

We drift through the gallery. There are so many striking pieces and different interpretations of the sea and coastline. I struggle to find one which I do not fall in love with. We do not speak. He seems suddenly distant and distracted. Although an unexplained distance has crept between us, he is still holding my hand, which I admit to liking. I enjoy the constant connection to him.

My eyes fix on a painting named *Oyster Catchers*. Around A4 in a white frame, it is smaller than some of the other paintings. It is of a beach where the tide has washed out. A small red fishing boat is beached on the shore, with seagulls rummaging through the sand and pebbles around it. It is beautiful if a little pensive in its mood. I tense, and he seems to have come back from wherever he had gone in his head.

"Are you okay?" He tightens his hand around mine.

I feel my eyes prick with tears, quickly wiping them away with my other hand, feeling ridiculous. "I'm fine, it just reminds me of my dad," I reply hurriedly, trying to get grip on myself.

"He fished?"

"Yes. I used to go out with him. The boat looks remarkably like the one he had, or at least how I remember it." I am still looking at the painting, aware he has turned and is looking at me.

"When did he die?"

The directness and perception of his question takes me by surprise. I turn to face him, and my eyes meet his. They are warm and his expression soft.

"When I was twelve. Heart attack. He had several and was in and out of hospital before the final one."

I cannot say the rest about the ache and hole he left in my heart. That he was my world, my solace and my escape from my mother and brother. That they hated him and continually belittled him. That the coronary report had concluded stress was a major contributor to his early death.

"I'm sorry." His tone is utterly sincere, as he continues to look at me, searching my eyes with his. "I think we're done here. Just give me a few minutes to arrange things with Judith."

From afar, I watch him chat with her. He seems relaxed and younger somehow while he is with her. He returns to me, and we are back in the bright sunshine outside.

"She was your teacher?" I ask.

"Yes, until she retired down here." His tone is cautious,

and he does not look at me. Maybe she is older than I thought.

"A-level?"

"Yes, though I never officially took A-level art."

It seems like an odd response, but I continue anyway. "What do you paint?"

"Mainly landscapes or seascapes. Sometimes people."

"Do you still paint?" I am intrigued by this side of him, which I would never have guessed in the short time I have known him.

"I don't have time, and it makes me melancholy." His tone is frigid and stilted.

I still cannot let it go. "Why not? Did you not want to pursue art?" My words come out wrong. Too nosey. Too direct.

He continues to avoid eye contact. "It's not what my father would have wanted or accepted." His tone is low now, dangerously low, which serves as a warning not to pursue this further.

With silence between us again, a chasm of awkwardness opens all around us. Looking at me as if the previous conversation never happened, he is the first to break it. He is smiling, but it does not reach his eyes. I know it is forced.

"So, lunch. There is a reasonable pub nearby, or what I consider to be the best fish and chips in Cornwall. You hungry? I do mean for food this time." He breaks into a grin, the tension appearing to be leaving him.

"Yes." I reply plainly. I am relieved he seems to be relaxing again. Maybe it is the sea air, but I am starving again.

He tilts his head to the side. Cute, very cute. "Any preference?"

I shake my head. "No, not really. Both sound good, but I guess it would be nice to eat outside on the beach maybe. It's such a beautiful day."

"Done." He beams, his mood now completely reversed.

He is warmer and happier again. It leaves me

contemplating the snippets of his life he clearly does not want me to go into.

CHAPTER THIRTEEN

We eat fish and chips on a small beach down below the gallery. It is empty, except for an occasional dogwalker. Off the beaten track for the usual tourist traffic, I guess. He is right. It is delicious. The fish is so fresh and lightly battered. He explains it is taken straight from the boat to the shop, which is why the menu is always determined by the catch of the day. The chips are chunky and full of flavour. My lips sting with the taste of vinegar and salt.

He leans back on his arms. He has discarded his boots and has buried his feet in the sand. "What do you think? Good, right?"

I nod, and he just smiles. We sit there for some time, watching the tide rolling in across the bay and crashing in small breakers. The seagulls cackle above us, hopeful for stray chips. The sun is bright and high in the sky, warm and balmy. I want to bottle the moment, completely relaxed and happy, not thinking about anything but here and now.

His voice breaks my train of thought. "Can I ask you a question?"

His tone is inexplicably serious, and I feel my anxiety rising instantly.

"You don't have to tell me," he continues.

"Okay," I reply hesitantly.

"When we were at the club you mentioned something about not being experienced. Last night about only having been with two. No, that's not right. One and a half people?"

He sounds like he does not really believe me. I nod. "That's right, I've only had sex with one other person and nearly sex once with someone else."

I know I am blushing and feel him reach for my hand, squeezing it gently in his.

"Nearly sex?" He raises his eyebrow quizzically. "Have you not wanted boyfriends? Was it a conscious thing, like a celibacy vow or something?"

I shake my head, dying of embarrassment. I would rather the ground opened up and swallowed me, than have to explain what had happened. How it had left me fearful of intimacy and repeating the near miss sexual experience, until now. That since then I had never wanted intimacy with anyone I had met in real life before I had met him. That until now this was the message I subconsciously gave off to anyone who attempted to get close to me in this way.

"Emily, look at me."

His voice is soft, but I still dread meeting his eyes. When I do, I find they are warm and gentle.

"You misunderstand me," he tells me. "It's not a criticism. I just think you're beautiful and very sexy. I'm struggling to see how it's even possible you were out there and decided to come home with someone like me. That's why I'm asking. You don't have to tell me. I just don't get how you haven't had guys queuing up to take you out." His voice is utterly sincere and calm.

I cannot hear him. I raise my eyebrow instead. Sarcasm has always been a good protection tool for me. "I know you're trying to be nice, Gabriel, but look at me. I'm hardly the catch of the year. I'm not the girl men approach on nights out or see as anything other than a friend."

He frowns. "I am looking at you. You just don't see yourself the way I do, or the way most men will see you. Curvy, sexy, beautiful, and that's just the physical. You're also kind, intuitive, and very smart. Scarily smart."

I blush fully, and he squeezes my hand once more. I tell him about James, my childhood sweetheart, who had been my best friend. The friend I had been in love with since starting secondary school and who finally decided I was worth dating when we both reached sixteen. I know in hindsight he manipulated me and generally put me down to make himself feel better, while he also dated another girl from a neighbouring school, as well as a few other girls on and off when we were at university, I also later discovered. When we finally did have sex, it was clinical and always on his terms, never exciting, loving or intimate. More just to tick a box. He always told me I was lucky he'd stuck with me for so long.

I continue to tell him about my failed sympathy sex at my work Christmas party. It comes blurting out how Richard told everyone I was frigid, that was the reason he could not get it up, and he was only doing me a favour as a friend anyway. He and his friends had then made sure the reputation followed me. With my mother's constant criticism, I guess I had just let it become my reality. It meant I had built walls around myself to protect me to stop anyone getting close enough to rub salt into these old, deep rooted wounds.

He listens intently, the frown on his face developing into a full-on scowl. "Fucking idiots. They sound delightful. You don't believe any of that shit surely?"

His anger surprises me. I bite my lip, looking back out to sea.

"Give me strength, Emily. If nothing else, I'm going to make it my personal mission to make you see this is complete bollocks."

I don't know how to respond. I don't believe him, however much I might want to. He sighs, and I look back at him. He shakes his head, standing up and pulling me with him. We stand awkwardly. Feeling vulnerable and exposed, I just don't know how to be after telling him all that. I still know so little about him.

Wrapping his hands around my waist, he pulls me against him, kissing me long and deep. He circles my tongue with his. He tastes deliciously of vinegar and salt.

"Beautiful Emily," he whispers as we pull apart.

We walk hand in hand back up the beach, towards the gallery. He swings his boots by the laces in his other hand, not putting them back on until we reach his car. I relax again on the drive back to Plymouth. We chat happily about his memories of spending time with his grandparents on their small holding near Polperro. He speaks about them with affection and love, about picking apples with his grandmother and learning to cook traditional Greek Cypriot dishes with his grandfather. We pull into the carpark at the back of the club. Within moments three men, one which I recognise to be Guy, come to the vehicle. Gabriel talks to them outside as they unload the paintings from the back of the Range Rover. When he gets back in, his mobile rings.

He looks at the screen and frowns. "Sorry, I need to take this."

His tone implies he really does not want to, but it makes no difference to me, and I shrug accordingly.

He hits the pick-up button. "What's up?" Whoever it is talks more than he does. He sounds annoyed when he answers. "No, I didn't forget. I've just had some business stuff today and got caught in traffic. We will drop by in a bit. Say half an hour."

The voice at the other end babbles some more.

He sighs. "Yes, we. See you in a bit." He hangs up and makes a face as he turns to me. "I promised to meet some people for a drink. Do you mind? We won't stay long."

I shake my head in response. Again, it makes no difference to me. I have no reason to object, vaguely intrigued by who his friends might be.

We drive towards Salcombe and stop at what looks to be a wine bar overlooking the bay by the water's edge. It has the air of being expensive and not a particularly relaxing place. The sign outside boasts an extensive shellfish and cocktail menu. He takes my hand once more and leads me to the roof terrace. Here he introduces me to two men, Toby and Henry, and three women, Arabella, Elsa, and Serena. I recognise them from the yacht. They are expensively dressed and well-groomed with superficial fixed smiles and scrutinizing, critical gazes. They all look me up and down as we approach. I feel immediately awkward and on edge.

"Can I get anyone a drink?" His hand still holds mine, but his whole demeanour has changed. The relaxed carefree mood from the beach has evaporated. His body is rigid, and his expression is cold and unsympathetic.

The woman he introduced as Serena steps forward. She is beautiful, with iridescent blue eyes and long platinum blonde hair which shines in the late afternoon sun. "Pimm's, darling. It's what we are all drinking."

I notice their glasses are still full. He nods, leaving me there as he walks back downstairs to the bar. Toby and Henry follow him.

"How long have you known Gabriel?" Serena's voice is clipped.

I know instantly she does not like me. "Not long." I answer vaguely.

She glares at me with cold indifference. "You're not fucking him then?"

The others snigger as I flounder, and she continues without waiting for a response. "Fucking Gabriel is not a huge achievement. He's not known for being particularly fussy, as anyone here will tell you, but you're not his usual type."

I want to say something bitingly sarcastic and know I will think of plenty of options later in hindsight. I also know if I try now, I will lose. "What does it matter to you?"

She smiles nastily. "Because it does. Ask him to explain it to you."

"Ask him what?" His voice is ice cold, but I am so glad he is back. His hand is warm on my lower back. He hands me a glass of Pimm's which I sip, glad to have something to do to distract me. I note he is holding a bottle of beer.

He smiles, but the ice does not thaw. "I hope you girls are playing nicely." His tone is deceptively playful and polite, but there is an unmistakable edge to it.

"Gabby, you know us. We always play nicely. We are just getting to know your new *friend*." Serena emphasises the word *friend* as if she has eaten something truly revolting. She leans forward and kisses him on both cheeks, her hand firmly placed on his arm.

She is so close I can smell her perfume. It is floral and musky. Gabriel physically tenses, and I wonder what the deal is between them. The apathy and unstated irritation roll off him in waves.

Continuing, she seems oblivious to his reluctance as she strokes his arm with her fingers. "It's been too long, Gabby. Father was asking whether I'd seen you recently. Apparently, you are doing some business with him."

I wonder why she calls him Gabby and whether it is his nickname. It sounds very preppy.

He shrugs, but her hand remains firmly in place on his arm. "Yes, I am arranging some shares for him." He sounds bored now.

"Father is so fond of you," Serena coos.

And so it continues. Painful small talk for the next twenty minutes or so. It feels much longer, before we make our excuses and leave.

"I'm sorry about that. They are rude and arrogant." He is not looking at me, but straight ahead at the road as he drives.

"It's not your fault. Are they your friends?" If they are honestly the people he chooses to spend his leisure time with, the thought fills me with dread.

"No, not friends. Just people I spend time with sometimes." His voice is flat.

"Is that not what a friend is?"

He laughs incredulously. "No, a friend is generally someone you like. I have three people I regard as friends. Two live in the States, the other is currently working as a doctor in Africa. These are people I am expected to be friends with. Our families are friends or business associates, so I tolerate it. What did Serena say to you?"

"She asked if I was fucking you and said you weren't fussy." My use of the F word surprises me.

He shakes his head. "Cheeky cow."

"She said to ask you why it mattered to her. What did she mean?"

He glances at me. "I'm supposed to be getting married to her when I turn thirty next year."

I almost choke. No wonder she wasn't keen on me. "You mean you're engaged to her?"

He laughs once more. "No, not even close. It's something our families would like to happen, as would Serena. I have always been very clear about my thoughts on it."

"Kind of like an arranged thing?" I manage to choke out.

"I guess."

"You're not going to do it then?" I breathe again.

He shrugs. "Maybe. I don't know. It's complicated. I've known Serena all my life, and we have no chemistry. She's very shallow, but it would be easy. Convenient, I guess."

That makes no sense at all, but then it dawns on me. "Oh, right. You're sleeping with her?"

He laughs more bitterly this time. "No, and I never have."

Something in his tone makes me not believe him. "Really,

Gabriel?" Is this anything to do with me? I am not sure why I need to know.

He grimaces. "She went down on me in the back of a limo a few years back. Said I should sample the goods and it would be the best I'd ever had. I think it was her way of sealing the deal, so to speak."

Urgh—too much information. The situation is getting worse.

"Was it? The best you've had, I mean." I do not know why, but I feel strangely jealous, not sure why any of this really matters to me.

He laughs again, without any joy. "No, definitely not."

"Why would you consider getting married? What if you met someone and fell in love?" Again, I wonder why I am asking. I am painfully aware it would unlikely be someone like me even in my wildest dreams.

Our eyes meet. His are cold and dark.

He looks away, back to the road. "You're assuming I believe in the concept of love."

"You don't?"

He does not answer.

"You must have had girlfriends though?" I press further. He has asked me after all.

He tightens his hands on the steering wheel. "Depends what you mean by girlfriend. Do you mean women I've had relationships with, or women I've fucked?" His voice is chillingly cold, unfamiliar and guarded.

I gulp. Maybe I should not have started this. "Is it a different number? Both, I guess, if so." Do I really want to know this?

"Yes, very different. I have had one relationship. I don't do them. I have never really wanted to commit to anyone, but I met someone not long after I came back from studying in the States. That's probably my one serious relationship. The only one I thought I actually wanted to spend a lifetime with. More than a few nights, anyway. This one was a while ago now. We were together just over a year, and it ended badly. Really bad. I've learnt from the mistake, and I don't allow people to get close to me. I'm pretty cold generally and not the nicest of people in reality. You just haven't seen that side of me yet." He pauses, and I note he has said *yet*. "I've fucked a lot of women. Too many, probably, but there it is. I've never pretended to be a saint."

"How many is a lot?" My head is spinning. I feel my anxiety rising. I think he is lovely, undeniably hot and smart but also caring and thoughtful from the little I have seen. Maybe it is just a very convincing, well-constructed act.

He raises an eyebrow and looks annoyed. "Does it matter?"

I do not answer. Does it matter? It is what it is, and I cannot change it, but something in me still wants to know. A lot tells me little and is subjective. A lot to me would be ten, maybe twenty. Somehow, I doubt this is the number we are looking at. We drive in silence a little way. The tension between us builds to a point it is almost claustrophobic. I do not think he is going to answer, which although curious, I am almost relieved about.

His voice shatters my contemplations. "I don't know. I don't remember everyone. I've not kept a journal, nor have I kept count, but it's got to be getting towards a couple hundred probably. I've spent a lot of nights in clubs. Mine and other peoples. I've not been in relationships so had no one to be loyal to or to answer to. As I said, I don't and won't do relationships. Or romance. Or any of that sentimental stuff. I'm not made for it. I know that now."

There it is. Stark and plain. I feel my mouth drop open. Has he been trying to work it out to give me an estimate in all this time? His tone implies he got hurt very badly, but he has said enough to make me not go there. A little part of me feels crushed and sad. I have no idea what I am doing here with him. His own description of himself is miles apart from how I would describe him. We had been having such a nice day, until now. It felt real and genuine. I worry I am setting myself up to get hurt. We travel the rest of the way in silence.

Chapter Fourteen

W hen we eventually pull up outside his house, all I want to do to is run and hide. I knew agreeing to come here in the first place was a bad idea. My head is confused. Why do I even care what he has said? What did I realistically expect? However much I try to ignore it, I do care. There is no point denying it. I like him, and he makes me feel special. He and whatever this is makes me feel alive. I need to remind myself none of this is real. That maybe, and with a very likely possibility, I do not really know him at all. I am a temporary distraction before his marriage. A bit of fun before whatever else is mapped out in his perfect life that he ends up doing. His future will not be with me. The thought depresses me further. My mood sours completely as I walk through the front door a little way in front of him.

Catching my hand in his, he spins me around. "Are you okay, Emily?" His face is more tender and has lost its fierceness.

I stand there motionless with no clue what to say. Clearly, I am not okay. I am struggling to understand it myself, let alone be in a position to articulate it.

He continues anyway as if my silence answers him. "I'm sorry. They bring out the worst in me, but it's no excuse. I was thoughtless. I shouldn't have said all of that in the car. I don't know why I even did. I would never normally discuss it. It was careless of me and rude. I talk far too easily with you. I forgot myself. I know I hurt you, and I really didn't want to do that."

I shake my head. "It's fine. Really. You were just being honest." I am not sure why I am trying to sound reasonable.

He frowns, his hand still holding mine. "No, it's not. I was a complete dick. I was really enjoying today with you. I want you to feel comfortable with me, not edgy and anxious like you are now. Tell me what you're thinking."

I flush red. Is it obvious how I am feeling? I have been advised several times by various acquaintances to never play poker. I hesitate. I do not want to think about my feelings for him, but there is more to this.

"I can never be like them, Gabriel. You and I are worlds apart. I knew it anyway, but . . . ." My words rush out on staccato.

He raises his hand to stroke my cheek stopping me midsentence. "Don't you see, this is exactly why I like spending time with you. Really like spending time with you." He pulls me into an embrace, his arms around me.

I close my eyes, and I can hear his heart beating through his shirt. I feel safe and comforted by the smell of him. In this moment, I can temporarily forget everything he has said. I can kid myself he is mine and we could somehow have a future together.

He pulls away, still holding me close, scrutinising me with concern etched on his face. "Can we start again, please? It's a beautiful evening and warm. I suggest we unwind in the hot tub and watch the sunset. How does that sound? It's what I would do if I was here on my own."

I do not quite believe him, but it does sound good. My body's tense, and my brain is still racing. Except for one thing. "I didn't bring a swimsuit."

He smiles mischievously. I know what he is thinking, but he appears to think better of it before he speaks. "Underwear is fine. It's behind tinted glass, so you can look out, but no one can see in."

"Ok, I guess. Oh, and should I be calling you Gabby?" I smile and ask more than a little sarcastically.

He rolls his eyes. "Christ. Please don't. I absolutely hate it."

He grabs what looks like a bottle of champagne from the fridge. I follow him outside, freezing by the hot tub. He undresses effortlessly down to black boxer shorts, like the Adonis he is, smooth tanned skin, muscles rippling. Inexplicably shy and uncomfortable, I know I will look far less elegant stumbling out of my clothes in front of him. He surveys me and frowns as if he is reading my mind. Turning, he steps into the hot tub with his back to me as he looks out across the ocean. I feel slightly ridiculous, hurriedly stripping down to my underwear. I am fully aware he has seen a whole lot more of me already, but I am still glad he has given me the quiet illusion of some privacy. He finds my eyes with his again, when I have submerged myself in the water.

He smiles his killer smile, the one which lights up his entire face, and hands me a glass of champagne. "I want you to relax. How would you relax at home?"

"I would read a book." I reply without hesitation, although the reality lately has been a very different story.

His smile widens. "Tell me about books and the stories which make you love literature. About the books you go back to time and time again."

I raise an eyebrow. "I think that would bore you rigid."

His smile softens, and his tone suddenly turns serious. "Nothing you say bores me."

We talk for the next hour or so about literature and the books I love or have inspired me. Woolf and Mansfield. Wilde and Bronte. Blake and Rossetti. Levin and Morrison. I enjoy talking to someone who appears to also love books, but at the same time challenges my opinions. The hot tub is relaxing. The champagne is dry and crisp. He moves me in front of him, massaging my shoulders with skill and precision. He loosens all the knots he finds there as we watch the sun dissolve back into the sky. Bringing his hands to rest on my stomach, he lets his fingers stretch out over my soft flesh as I lean back against him. I am calm and rejuvenated.

"Am I forgiven?" he whispers in my ear, his tone low and seductive.

"Yes," I half murmur.

He wraps his legs around me and strokes my stomach with his hands, which gives me butterflies. His fingers move up across my breasts, gently massaging as he cups and teases them. I turn to face him in the swirling water, and he finds my lips with his. I wrap my legs around him as we continue to kiss. I can feel his erection growing against me through my knickers. Without warning, he lifts me so I am sitting on the edge of the tub. My back is against the glass wall, which is warm from the late evening sun. He kisses my neck, then moves down my chest and circles his tongue around my nipples. They are pink and swollen as he alternates between them. I want to scream, the feeling is so pleasurable and intense.

He locks his mischievous gaze on mine as he moves down, kissing my stomach until he is at the top of my knickers. Kneeling up, he pulls back, loops his fingers on either side of the lacy fabric, pulls them down my legs, and throws them to one side. He smiles wickedly, nudging my legs apart. I am completely accessible to him. He still kneels in front of me. The frothing bubbles surround his torso and my legs.

"So pretty," he whispers.

Embarrassed being so intimately observed by him, I do not have long to dwell on it. He rests his hands on my thighs, holding my legs apart as he kisses my stomach once more, before finding the bud of my clitoris, which he greets with single long lick. The sensation is unfamiliar and unexpected. As he does it again, my nerve endings come alive as if everything is hot-wired between my legs. One of his hands strokes between my legs, pulling my pubic hair gently upwards to gain access to my most private parts. He licks once more with a long, slow stroke of his tongue, circling my clitoris until it throbs before sucking gently. The feeling is intimate and exquisite. I hold the edge of the tub trying to steady myself. I want to close my legs to control the intensity, but his hands hold me in place. He slows his pace, finding my eyes with his once more. His expression is lustful between my thighs as he moves his hands back up my body to gently pinch my nipples.

"You taste as good as I imagined." His voice is dark and husky now.

He sucks more forcefully, but it is what I want. His fingers move inside me, and I arch my back against the wall. I groan softly. Any embarrassment has long since dissipated. It is lost in the moment and the sensation.

"My greedy girl, I don't have enough hands," he murmurs.

He takes my hands and smiles as he spreads my fingers out on my breasts under his own while he teases my nipples. I have never touched myself like this. It feels naughty, but so good. I knead the flesh of my breasts as his fingers re-enter me. He rubs my clitoris with his thumb until he replaces it with his tongue. His gaze does not leave mine while I continue to play with my nipples, unable to look away even if I wanted to. He licks my clitoris before dipping lower to the swollen lips of my vulva, which he continues to penetrate with his fingers. Rolling his tongue, he builds me to the point that I can think of nothing but him.

My hips buck. I feel everything inside me explode, floating away on waves of pleasure I have only discovered in the last couple of days. His mouth is still between my legs, tasting and exploring — as are his fingers, but more slowly now at a leisurely pace as I catch my breath. Every feeling is heightened, and I feel utterly turned on.

He sits up, pulling me on top of him so I am kneeling over his lap, holding me in position and steadying me. I reach down and ease his boxer shorts off his hips, releasing his huge erection. It is rigid and thick between my legs, against my belly. He smiles up at me with an almost innocent expression. I raise up, reaching down and guiding him inside of me until he fills me completely.

"You're in control, Emily." He continues to look up at me. Still I can see an innocence, almost a vulnerability in his face.

I am truly in control, in this position. I can ride him as fast or slowly as I like. I begin to move, rolling my hips and getting used to him being inside me. I can feel his wiry pubic hair between my legs. I rock against him, rubbing my clitoris against his pubic bone as he sucks my nipples. His erection grows even harder. He stretches into me as I hold the edge of the tub to steady myself. I know he is close as I continue to roll my hips down on him. He throws his head back. His breathing is ragged. I do not stop. Instead, I push down on him and force him deeper inside me. My clitoris throbs and quivers as I clench around him furiously. We both erupt into a long, intense climax. He pulls me close against him, burying his face against my chest. The aftershocks move between us, and his erection slowly ebbs away.

Eventually he looks up. He is smiling with no hint of stress or distraction. "Beautiful, beautiful, Emily." With seeming reluctance, he pulls away. "I have to work for a little bit."

He lifts me to the side, standing. He stoops down, kissing my forehead, before leaving me in the dancing bubbles. I watch as he walks naked through the house, thinking through the events of today. I wonder which is the real Gabriel and if I will ever really know.

CHAPTER FIFTEEN

I lie there in the bubbles for a little while longer as the sky darkens. Eventually the hot tub switches off automatically, and the outside lights illuminate all around me. I plod into the house following his wet footsteps upstairs, surprised at my lack of inhibitions and the feeling of freedom in my own nakedness. I do not think I could feel any better in this moment.

I check my phone and see the daily *fine* response text from my mother. It is quickly followed by another which says *wasting away.* I smile a little. Some things never change, which has a reassuring familiarity. Other aspects of my life could not be more different currently. I run a long hot bath, feeling suddenly quite cold. I wash the light chlorine from my body and hair, redressing in a black silk robe I find hanging behind the door.

As I move back into the bedroom, I see a rectangular, flat parcel wrapped in silver tissue paper with huge purple ribbons. The accompanying card simply says Emily. The writing is curved and flamboyant, almost like calligraphy. Instinctively, I know it is his. I open the parcel, inquisitive and genuinely excited. It is the painting from the gallery. The one which made me well up like a baby. My eyes prick with tears again, but with happiness. His words, "I don't do romance or sentiment" ring in my ears. My phone beeps. It is Lucy.

I start to reply, then decide it would be easier to speak, and besides we usually speak at least once every day.

She answers on the first ring, slightly out of breath "Everything okay?"

"Yes, everything is great." Now that I'm speaking to my best friend, I am lost for what to say.

"Is that it?" Lucy sighs. "Seriously, what's been happening? Is everything good?"

I pause. "Yes, amazing. He's amazing." Which is true, except for all the things I do not know and he does not discuss.

"Oh — my — God! Have you been to bed yet?"

I feel myself blush. "A few times."

Lucy nearly chokes. "I'm not even going to ask if he's any good. His reputation's more than enough. Wow. So, are you guys dating?"

"No." I shake my head. "I don't think so. He doesn't do relationships."

"Stop it. And why not?"

"He's been screwed over in the past."

"If he doesn't do relationships, he's obviously not been seeing the right people. Try food and sex — works on most men! Sorry, babe, got to run. There's someone at the door. Ring me back soon."

I lie back on the bed. Neither of us are likely to be particularly hungry, given the amount of food we have eaten today. And sex? Well, he is far more experienced than me. What could I realistically do? In a rushed moment of clarity, it hits me.

In the kitchen, I find a bottle of brandy on the wine rack by the fridge and pour two glasses. I neck mine fast, before refilling the glass. I walk back downstairs in the direction of his study. It is not like the rest of the house. Dark wood panels line the walls. To one side is a huge desk that looks antique, with thick wooden legs and a high-backed leather chair. He glances at me over his glasses, from his laptop as I enter. He looks different in this setting. A little fierce and almost intimidating. I begin to doubt my plan.

"Sorry, I didn't mean to interrupt you. I wondered if you

had nearly finished." My words rush out, not quite the sexy siren I am aiming for.

"I will be working for some time yet, but I am due a break." His voice is calm and even, but there is a definite chill in it. He moves his laptop to the side and removes his glasses.

I decide to ignore the seeming coldness in in his mood. Instead, I move closer towards him, handing him his drink.

He takes a large swig. "Is everything okay?"

I down my drink as he watches me. "I wanted to say thank you for the painting. It was really lovely of you, and I wanted to try something."

"You're welcome, though I am not very lovely. What did you want to try?" His tone is cautious. He watches me with an expression of curious fascination now.

I lean into him and kiss him, running my tongue along his lips, then dipping into his mouth. It surprises him, but he responds quickly. I run my hands through his hair, which is wet. He must have showered. The smell of limes and sandalwood greets me. He tastes vaguely of mint, mixed with brandy. I pull away, and he fixes his eyes on me. Nowhere to run.

"What did you want to try?" His voice has dropped. It is low and husky, the way I know it is when he is turned on.

I unbutton his shirt clumsily, exposing his chest. I shower his warm skin with butterfly kisses as I move down his abdomen until I am kneeling between his legs. I look up, and he continues to train his eyes on me. His raises one eyebrow, questioning. I undo his fly and reach inside his jeans. His penis grows in my hands under the soft fabric of his boxers, and his breathing hitches slightly. I reach up and tug at the waist band, unsuccessfully trying to move his jeans down. A smile flickers across his face as he lifts his hips to make it easier. I pull them down with his boxers, freeing his growing erection which is at my eye level. I run my hand up and down his penis, stroking and caressing him. His erection grows in my fingers as I watch.

I run my tongue the full length of him from the base to the tip. His skin is smooth and soft. I circle my tongue around the head. Looking up, I see his eyes are hooded as he focuses them on me. His expression is intrigued as he bites his bottom lip. I circle the head again with my tongue. His breathing quickens. He is enjoying this. I open my mouth wide and take him in. Sucking down on him like a lollipop, I roll my tongue around the head of his penis intermittently. He is flushed, moving his hips slowly, like he is trying to be restrained. I take him further into my mouth and throat, sucking hard. His hands fist in my hair. His erection strengthens as his penis probes my mouth. I am surprised how much I am enjoying the sensation. I am enjoying giving and controlling his pleasure. I open my mouth wider to take him further in.

"Emily, stop. Stop or I'm going to come." He steadies my head with his hands.

I slow, glancing up at him. He is utterly flushed, and I know I have him. I circle the tip of his penis once more with my tongue.

"Fuck, Emily. I'm serious. Stop, or I'm going to come in your mouth." His voice is strained.

It is taking all his effort to hold back. I pull his hands from my head, and I hold them still on the arm rests of his chair while taking him deep into my mouth. We still lock our gazes on each other. I suck harder on him, and he rolls his hips. He throws his head back, and I know he is close. His penis is solid as rock and throbbing between my lips. He murmurs my name, and he comes as I continue to pleasure him. He fills my mouth in waves with warm saltiness.

I look up, and he is watching me once more. His expression is difficult to read. His breathing is ragged. He stands, dragging up his jeans, but leaves them undone. He pulls me up into his arms. Kissing me, he pushes my mouth open with his. Undoing my robe with one tug of the sash, he exposes my naked body, which he runs his eyes over greedily. We stand close together, so close my body already aches for him.

"Okay, without doubt, that was the best blowjob I've ever had."

His voice is deep and hushed. His tone is genuine, leaving me in little doubt he means it. I glow with quiet pride, desperate to feel his hands on me again.

He observes me shrewdly, narrowing his eyes. "Who have you been practising on, you naughty girl?"

I start to protest. As our eyes meet, I know he does not seriously think I have been practising on someone else. We are playing a new game, and I have yet to learn the rules.

"No one, Gabriel. I just wanted to do something for you to say thank you," I manage to say.

"No one? Is that anyway to address me?" His eyes are ice cold and commanding.

I pause. The realization dawns on me from a previous conversation. I understand part of the game now. "No, sir."

A smile flickers across his face, and he narrows his eyes further. "Better. You must understand, if you come into my study and unman me in this way, you belong to me to do with as I please. For my pleasure. Do you understand?" His voice is utterly calm, but there is a cold edge to it. His mood is dangerous and domineering. He continues to penetrate my eyes with his, without compromise.

A quiver of nervous excitement moves through me. "Yes, sir."

He lifts me so I am sitting on his desk. The papers he was working on are now underneath me or cascading onto the floor. He kisses me hard again, pushing between my legs. His jeans rub against me like he did in the club. This time I am naked except for the robe around my shoulders. It leaves me expectant and wanting more. I lift my legs higher around him. He knows I am turned on. I know it is deliberate as he grinds against me, pulling my body against his.

He steps back and pulls my legs further apart until my feet rest against the heavy wooden legs of his desk.

Pulling the sash away from the gown, he smiles, kneeling and tying my feet in place. Standing back, still smiling, he takes in the view. I flush with heat, acutely aware my legs are spread-eagled on his desk. The wood is cold and hard against the bare skin on my thighs. I am desperate for him to touch me. He stares between my legs with such intensity I can almost feel myself becoming wetter.

All I can hear is the faint sound of the sea lapping on the shoreline in the distance. He smiles once more as he moves towards me. I think he is going to kiss me, but he does not. Instead, he knots one hand into my hair, pulling my head to one side so he can kiss my neck. He does so with a slight nip, sending a pulse of electricity through my arched body. Moving down to my nipples, he bites them on the line somewhere between pleasure and pain. It makes me squeal before he returns them to the soft wetness of his mouth. He alternates between his teeth and his tongue until my nipples are swollen and erect.

I am utterly consumed by him, completely absorbed in the moment as he drops to his knees. He sucks hard at my clitoris. None of the gentleness of earlier. Forceful and without restraint. Occasionally he grazes over my skin with his teeth, as he pushes two fingers into me. He follows with a third, while he continues his assault on my clitoris with his tongue. Waves of pleasure move through me as he winds me up tighter and tighter. Every time he suspects I may be close to release he slows, leaving me frustrated in some sweet torture. I want to bring my legs together but am unable to. He continues to explore me with his fingers. I roll my hips against him trying to increase the friction. He bites at my nipples and at my breasts once more. My nipples harden further as he blows gently over them. The cool air from his breath chases the sting away, until I do not think I can take it any longer.

"My greedy girl," he chides. "You will not come until I let you. Do you understand?"

I nod, not sure if I will be able to stop myself.

He sighs. "I don't have enough hands or fingers to pleasure you it seems, for the second time today."

Thrusting his fingers deep inside me once more, he makes me gasp. He withdraws them, leaving me empty and missing the fullness. Leaning over me, he reaches for two small rubber edged bulldog clips from the desk, grinning widely. I know what he intends. He clips one to my swollen nipple and pauses, looking at me with questioning eyes, gauging my reaction and whether this is okay. It pinches. The weight pulls down on my nipple slightly as he tugs gently, but the feeling is pleasurable, which I am embarrassed to admit. I nod in agreement. He smiles and does the same with the other nipple, still watching me. I nod once more, watching him. He tugs the clips gently on both nipples, heightening the pinch and sending shockwaves down my body. He buries his face between my legs, sucking and licking with an intense ferocity. I can only think about him, as I struggle to try to control the sensations. My body quivers toward its release.

He stops without warning and stands, wiping his hand across his mouth and taking a long sip of brandy. He locks his gaze back on mine. Everything between my legs is wet and swollen, but also cold. I am utterly on show to him. Nowhere to hide. The bulldog clips still swing from my nipples, keeping my senses heightened. I want him inside me so badly it almost hurts. I know he knows but is enjoying making me wait.

He takes another mouthful of brandy. "What do you want,

Emily?"

"You, Gabriel." I do not hesitate. My voice is breathless. Never have I wanted someone the way I want him in that moment.

He raises an eyebrow in response, cold and utterly in control.

I correct myself. "You, sir."

"Which part of me would you like?" His voice remains calm, but his expression is slightly fierce.

"Your pe-penis, sir," I stammer. This is unfamiliar to me. The anticipation is excruciating.

"Where would you like my cock, Emily?" He moves towards me and runs his fingers along my cheek across my lips before inserting one into my mouth.

Instinctively I suck it. I taste myself, salty and slightly metallic.

"Would you like my cock back in your mouth, Emily?" He half smiles.

I continue to suck his finger. I am his utterly.

He removes his finger from my mouth and runs it down my body to between my legs. "Or would you like my cock in your tight greedy pussy?"

Before I can answer, he runs his fingers down under my bottom, stroking my anus gently, which makes me shudder. The sensation is completely alien, but surprisingly pleasurable.

He smiles knowingly. "Or in your ass, Emily?"

I nearly choke. I can barely speak, and he smiles. He looks so hot, but also the utter bad boy. So very in control.

"My pussy, sir," I confirm.

"Your greedy little pussy. Are you sure?" As he speaks, he continues to glide his finger over my anus. His thumb is stroking my clitoris now, which throbs beneath his touch. It feels so wrong but so erotic at the same time.

"Yes, sir."

He circles his finger once more, and I quiver shamelessly.

"Okay, but I will have all of you. As I said, you belong to me now, as does your pleasure. All of your pleasure." He removes his hand, stepping back and pushing his jeans off his hips.

His erection seems even larger than earlier, almost angry. He moves towards me like a lion stalking its prey. He enters me with a single uncompromising thrust, filling me completely, while he gently pulls the clips on my nipples and circles his hips. I writhe around him, trying to find some release. He removes the clips, rolling my nipples between his fingers as the blood returns to them. They tingle and throb beneath his stroking fingers, which he runs over my breasts as he thrusts between my legs. I rise my hips to meet him, unable to wrap my legs around him.

"Come for me, Emily," he half whispers.

I never would have imagined him saying that would have any impact, but I unravel beneath him. His pace does not slow this time. He continues to tease my nipples as my clitoris rubs against his pubic bone. Everything clenches between my legs, carrying me away with unbelievable pleasure and much-needed release. Pulling me against him in his arms, he kisses me as I continue to orgasm. Still moving deep inside me, his erection is rigid and firm. I know we are far from finished. Stroking my body, he pushes me back on the desk. With my hands behind me, he rides me again, strong and fast. He thrusts his penis in and out with a fury which makes my swollen sex ache. I have no chance of keeping up with his pace. Arching my back, I feel like I am melting into him. He roams his hands over me and rests them under my bottom, tilting my hips upwards to gain even deeper access. I hear myself scream his name as my body explodes around him. He continues to ride me through floods of orgasm. Each surge is more intense than the last as he too reaches his climax. We writhe together, tangled with each other, until we are both utterly sated. I lie back on the desk barely able to move. My whole body is tingling and exhausted. He unties my ankles, wraps me in the gown still hanging on my arms, and carries me back upstairs.

CHAPTER SIXTEEN

"Emily."

I hear his voice in my sleep. Low and soft. Am I dreaming?

"Emily, babe, wake up."

I open my eyes reluctantly and squint as they adjust to the light hitting them. It is still dark outside. The bedside lamps are on, and he is sitting on the edge of the bed. I go to sit up and see I am only dressed in the gown from earlier, which gapes open. My nipples and vagina are sore. I flush with embarrassment as the memories of what we have done come back to me. Disorientated, I pull the covers up around me. I am in his bed, which confuses me further. Are we still playing this game in roles? I glance at him and see he is fully dressed in jeans and a dark grey sweater. He's wearing his glasses, as if he has been working.

"Emily." He speaks more forcefully now.

I focus my eyes on him properly. The expression he wears is not fierce and commanding, but soft and concerned. My head is a complete muddle. I am still lost somewhere between sleep and consciousness.

"Emily. I need to talk to you."

It hits me. "What's wrong?"

He reaches for my hand under the covers, and my anxiety rises. "It's your mother. She's had a fall, and she's in the hospital. They're saying they will need to operate."

"What? But how? I don't understand." My head spins, and I start to flounder.

"I don't know, babe. I'm sorry. Lucy rang the club, and they rang me. That's all they said. You didn't hear your phone. It's charging in your room. I didn't think." He sounds mortified and regretful.

My breathing quickens. "I have to go. I have to be there. Please, can you ring a taxi for me?"

He strokes my hand under the cover, shaking his head. "I know, and I will take you. I've put some clothes in the bathroom for you. Grab a quick shower, and I'll make some coffee."

"There isn't time." I cannot think straight. My only priority is to get to the hospital in this moment.

"Emily, please. We'll be out of here in twenty minutes. I need you to wake up and calm down, if you can. To get your head together." His voice is soft and soothing.

I'm shaking. I pull my hand from his, wrapping my arms around me.

He kisses my forehead gently as he stands. "Please, babe. I'll be in the kitchen."

The shower barely registers. I feel panicked and numb. It makes no sense. Mother is bed bound, and there are lots of measures in place to keep her safe. I feel disgusted with myself I was not there. Disgusted when I think what I was doing when she needed me and when this was probably happening. Where was David in all of this and what was he doing? The Carers always raise the bed sides before they leave on the last call. Mother cannot lower them herself. Had they forgotten? The questions swirl around my head, consuming me in a confused mess. I pull on the jeans he has left on the bed for me with a jumper. It is one of his, and I am glad of its warmth and reassurance as I pull it over my head. The sleeves are long on me. I push them up my arms. It feels cold, really cold. I am not sure if it is me or the chill of early morning. Defeated, I plod into the kitchen.

He turns immediately and hands me a lidded thermos cup. "Here. Ready to go?"

I nod and follow him out of the house. The cup warms my hands, but the rest of me is still freezing. There is no noise, just the sound of the engine running. I take a sip from the cup. Chai latte, like I occasionally order from the shop. Sweet and heady with cinnamon and cardamom. It strikes me how thoughtful that is. Momentarily, I am distracted by the fact he even remembered. It is still dark. The sun is just beginning to rise and break through the darkness. I have forgotten to put my watch on and have no idea of the time.

We pull up outside the hospital, and I shudder. I hate it here. It reminds me of my dad when he was ill. I wonder if anyone has happy memories of visiting this hospital and am absorbed by my memories. I do not hear him open the passenger door.

"You okay, Emily?"

His voice startles me. I look up and see his hand outstretched. "You're coming in?" That surprises me further and is unexpected.

He nods. "Yes, of course, unless you would rather I didn't."

Of course, I want him to stay. I am scared of what I am walking into and fearful about what is going to happen. I take his hand, still surprised he is not just dropping me off.

The smell of bleach and antibacterial handwash hits me as soon as we walk in the main entrance. I have no idea where we are going, but he clearly does. We enter the first available lift, and he hits the button for C floor. He asks at the reception desk. The nurse flutters her eyelashes at him unashamedly as if I am invisible beside him. She pushes her ample chest out as she stands to point us in the right direction. We walk to the end of the corridor, past all the wards still in semi-darkness with slumbering bodies in cubicles, until we find a small side room at the end.

Lucy jumps up immediately, throwing her arms around me. "I came in to make sure you weren't on your own and for support," she whispers in my ear.

David scowls as he stands. "Bothered to show up?"

Gabriel steps forward, his hand brushing mine as he stands by my side. "We only got the call a little while ago. It's my fault. Emily was not with her phone." His voice is utterly calm and even.

David stands close in front of me. I can smell the cigarette smoke on his clothes and pear drops on his breathe.

"Busy, were you?" he sneers, glaring at Gabriel. "I can imagine with this renowned lothario. I assume this is who I think it is?"

"How did she fall?" I stammer, hating the way I am letting him intimidate me as always.

"Out of bed," he snaps.

"The Carers always put the cot sides up." It makes no sense. Had they forgotten on this occasion? Had he not checked on her?

"Obviously, not on this occasion." David can barely contain his outrage. "If you had been there, doing your job this would not have happened. You should be utterly ashamed."

"Now's really not the time." Gabriel's voice remains calm, but there is an edge to it.

"You get an opinion, do you, Mr. Hunter-Law?" He spits the words in Gabriel's direction, whilst maintaining his focus on me. "Enjoy it while it lasts, Emily. You're a complete tramp. Men like this are only interested in one thing. He'll soon get bored with you and move onto the next tart. You'll come home snivelling with your tail between your legs. Only you won't this time."

I want the ground to open up and swallow me with embarrassment and shame. I do not understand what he is saying, and I do not care at this point. I have no energy left to process his words.

"Enough." I hear the tension in Gabriel's voice now, carefully controlled anger. "I may not be entitled to an opinion on your mother, but I am where Emily is concerned. I won't have you speak to her like that."

David grins nastily. "Really? What are you going to do about it?"

Clearly exasperated, Gabriel sighs. "Keep going and try me. I suggest you stop being such an infant and focus on what's important here."

David flushes red, his fists clenched at his side. Before he can respond, a doctor enters the room.

"Hello. I am Dr Mackenzie." She is tall, blonde and striking. "Are you the daughter, Emily?"

I nod, and she continues. "I am sorry we are not meeting in better circumstances. We have taken your mother into surgery. She has internal bleeding from her spleen and has shattered her hip along with her thigh bone. She appeared very frail on presentation here. We wanted to ask you and your brother about some bruising on her collarbone and back."

"It will be from the fall," David counters.

"No, it is a couple of days old, we think. Not to worry now if you are not aware. The surgery will take some time. I will be back to advise on the progress." Doctor Mackenzie's voice is kind and measured, but my instinct tells me not to be completely fooled by this as she leaves the room.

David is visibly seething. I do not know why, but I am reminded of my pet rabbit which he kicked against the garden fence when we were children. We all sit down again in silence. Gabriel is on one side of me, holding my hand. Lucy is on the other side, leaning into me. They flank me like personal bodyguards.

"You can go, Gabriel," I whisper. "I know you probably have meetings."

He shakes his head. "I'm not going anywhere unless you'd rather I did." He finds my eyes with his. They are utterly warm, and his expression is full of concern, clear and genuine.

I do not need to answer.

He nods. "I just need to make a couple of calls to rearrange my day. Lucy, are you okay to stay with Emily until I get back? I'm assuming the shop is open today."

She nods and looks taken aback. "Yeah, sure, of course."

He leaves the room, mobile in hand.

Lucy puts her arms around me. I barely feel it, like I am a million miles away from her.

"Okay, so he's not at all what I was expecting, very attentive and very in control," she whispers, and I smile weakly at her obvious swoon.

Gabriel returns quickly, exchanging numbers with Lucy before she heads into work. We sit for most of the morning, and he does not leave my side. He tucks me under his arm, trying to convince me to rest, which I do not. The consultant comes back briefly to tell us Mother is out of surgery but yet to regain consciousness. David's wife, Verena, arrives mid-morning in a bluster of peach and *Anais Anais.* I wonder where the children are but think better than to ask. The hours tick by as I watch the hands crawl around the clock on the wall. I wonder idly who the last family were to sit in this room.

The consultant drifts back in. "Your mother is conscious." Her tone is unreadable, but there is a hint of relief in it.

We all stand up, like soldiers to attention.

She turns to look at me, her expression one of pity. "Miss Black, I am sorry, but she has asked for you not to be admitted, and we must respect the patient's wishes."

"You're not welcome, Emily," my brother sneers spitefully.

It occurs to me he probably knew this was going to happen.

"Mother will be moving to a nursing home near Verena

and I, as soon as she is discharged."

My head spins once more. I feel numb and empty, vulnerable and alone. "What have you done? She would never agree to go into a home. She has always been really clear, and she would hate it." I can hear the despair in my voice.

He grins smugly. "Well, she has. She has given me power of attorney over all her assets including the house. The arrangements have been made. She realises now you have not been looking after her properly."

It all clicks into place in my head. "That's why you came isn't it? For the money. That's why you always come."

His grin does not falter. "I expect all of your things to be gone the day after tomorrow or they'll be taken to the tip. I also expect you to clear and pack up the house to make it market ready."

"No, you can't do this." I feel the tears welling in my eyes, but I refuse to let him see me cry.

"I already have."

I feel the sticky liquid hit my face and hair before it registers that he has thrown the remainder of whatever was in his cup at me. The cup itself hits me and falls crumpled by my feet. The consultant looks horrified as David and Verena leave the room. She follows shortly afterwards with the mutterings of apologies. I stand there utterly lost and humiliated. Gabriel places his arm around my shoulder. He ushers me from the room past a waiting cleaner, who looks at me with a mixture of curiosity and amusement.

Gabriel pulls me tight against him, the warmth of his body pouring into mine. "Let's go home, Emily."

Chapter Seventeen

I do not remember getting into the car or driving back to his house. He opens the car door and half carries me inside. I feel like I have shut down. Everything sounds like it is a little distance away. It is like I have left my body and am observing someone else's life. All I can smell is the sweet, milky coffee which is stuck to my hair and skin, down my back and chest. I feel sick. He leads me to the bathroom in his room and sits me on the chair by the bath.

"Emily, I'm going to run you a bath and find you some clean clothes. Okay?" His voice is quiet.

I nod my head, the tears rolling down my cheeks once more. He does not comment. Instead he turns on the water. When he returns, he places some clean clothes a little way from me on the floor as he leaves. I do not move. I sit there in complete inertia. Eventually, I get into the water, sitting there looking at the bubbles whirl around me. The water is warm and scented, but it does little to soothe me.

David came just for the money, and I was too stupid to see it. The money has never interested me, and I have never asked for anything. She has always said she would rather die than go into a nursing home. I am homeless and staying with a man I have known for less than a week. She has bruises a few days old. The thoughts swirl around in my head as if my brain is in a washing machine on full spin. I feel cold, really cold, hearing a knock at the door.

"Emily, are you okay? You've been in there a really long time?" he asks gently.

Have I? I do not have any sense of time. He walks in cautiously as if he is not sure what he is going to find or whether he should be intruding.

He puts his hand in the water and then on my shoulder. "Shit, Emily. It's freezing. You're freezing."

He turns on the hot tap. The warmth begins to return to my feet as I wriggle my toes.

Reaching for a sponge, he rubs it gently over my back. "Put your head back."

He proceeds to wash my hair, rinsing the suds and applying conditioner before brushing through the tangles left by the syrupy liquid. He is incredibly gentle and tender. I feel like a child, helpless but cherished. He pulls the plug and wraps me in a large fluffy towel before handing me the clothes he has pulled out. Pyjama bottoms and a long-sleeved jersey top, which I think is his. I follow him back into his room and sit on the bed, not sure where to be or how to be. Everything is just numb.

"Are you hungry?" His voice startles me from my thoughts.

I shake my head. Food is the last thing I want.

He sighs but does not pursue it. "Okay. You should get some sleep though. Try to at least get some rest." His voice is still calm and soothing, but more authoritative now.

I look out the window, and I am surprised to see the sun is going down. It is later than I thought.

"I don't want to be on my own," I blurt out, standing to go to my room, feeling defeated and very alone. My voice sounds alien to me as the tears continue to roll silently down my face.

He smiles gently. "Hey, no, stay in here. Stay if you want. I can work on the bed next to you."

I do want that, though I do not think I will sleep. As my head hits the pillow, the last thing I remember is him pulling the covers up and around me.

I wake the next morning, disorientated and slightly dizzy with no idea where I am. Gradually I come round and see I am in Gabriel's bed. The sun is streaming in through the windows. He is sitting beside me, tapping on his laptop, and stops when he sees I am awake.

"How are you feeling?" he asks cautiously.

"Okay, I think. Numb." I feel exhausted and strangely detached, like I am outside looking in.

He nods as if he understands. "I'll get some coffee."

I lie back on the bed, still trying to get my head together. I hear a doorbell and muffled voices. One I make out to be Gabriel's. He sounds irritated.

He strides back into the bedroom, clearly annoyed. "Emily, the police are here, and they have a few questions to ask you."

"What?" Any composure I had started to find disappears, and I fall down the rabbit hole once more.

"Nothing to worry about." His voice soothes, almost convincingly. "Just routine apparently."

I follow him into the kitchen, acutely aware I must look a complete state in mismatched pyjamas with bed hair. I have not seen myself in a mirror, but I know my eyes will be swollen and red. Two police officers are standing there. A petite blonde woman in uniform and a young man in a green suit, with dark, gelled back hair.

"Miss Black?" The male officer steps forward. His voice lacks any emotion.

"Yes." My voice sounds small and unfamiliar to me. I feel dizzy again and overwhelmed with guilt for no reason.

"We are sorry to disturb you at this time, but we have a few questions about your mother we need to get out of the way so the matter can be concluded." He pauses giving me time to process what he has just said. "You were living with her as her primary carer?"

I nod in response.

"For how long?"

"About nine months. We also have Carers from the Council who come in four times a day." My voice falters slightly.

He nods. "Yes, we have spoken to them. You have not been staying there this week?"

I shake my head. "My brother has been. I was not needed."

"Emily has been staying here. As I already explained." Gabriel sounds really annoyed, verging on angry.

The officer nods again. "Yes, I know, but we have to establish the facts and what has happened."

"Can I ask why?" I sound more confident than I feel, but it occurs to me I am answering questions with no idea why they are here.

The police and Gabriel all stare at me. It makes me feel even more uncomfortable if that was humanly possible. Something new occurs to me. "Are you investigating me?" I ask.

"No, Miss Black, we are not. We are trying to establish what happened the night your mother fell. The Care Agency was clear the cot sides were raised, but they were lowered when paramedics were called to the property. Your mother's arthritis means she herself could not have lowered them. The Care Agency have also raised concerns she seemed intoxicated and confused. In addition, although of apparently sound mind, she has signed a power of attorney agreement relinquishing control of her assets. She has unexplained bruising which the hospital has raised safeguarding alerts for. All of which means we are obliged to investigate." The male police officer's voice is pragmatic and ice cold.

"I don't understand what you're trying to tell me." My head continues to spin, and I feel faint.

I wonder if I look it. Gabriel's arm slips around my waist as if he senses I am about to fall. I feel pathetic. I am being pathetic. What on earth is going on? I have nothing to feel guilty about or I need to justify, but I feel ashamed. Ashamed about what I was doing when all of this happened, but I did not cause it.

"We are investigating potential abuse and neglect, both financial and physical."

The female officer elaborates, breaking my chain of thought. The blood rushes to my head. My heart pounds in my chest and echoes in my ears. I think I am going to be sick.

"You are aware of her brother's financial situation? He is on the verge of bankruptcy," Gabriel interjects. His voice cuts through the air like a knife.

How does he know about David's financial situation? I have no idea. Things begin to make even less sense in my head. I knew there were problems. Verena spends money like water, but bankruptcy?

The male officer nods. "Yes, Mr. Hunter-Law, we are aware. To be clear, Miss Black, as I said, we are not investigating you, but we need to establish the facts and are tying up loose ends."

"You think my brother did this?" Of course, they do. I do in reality, but I barely dare to say it out loud.

"I cannot comment. Either way it is unlikely we will get very far with any investigation. To be honest, cases like this are notoriously difficult to prove and your mother is being . . ." He grimaces, like he is looking for the right words. "Is not being very cooperative. We will leave you to it. Thank you for your time."

Gabriel walks them to the door, deep in hushed conversation, before returning to my side. "Are you okay?" His voice is softer now and brooding.

"I'm so sorry I brought this into your home, Gabriel." I really am. Talk about baggage.

"You didn't, babe. None of this is your fault." He kisses my head gently, pulling me to him. I feel safe again, safe in the warmth of his embrace.

He encourages me to eat breakfast, though I have no appetite. I eat half a banana and some yogurt to appease him, with lots of coffee. The coffee I gladly accept, welcoming the caffeine hit to make me feel less tired. I feel like I am sleepwalking through the day, although I am fully awake.

We spend the afternoon walking along the cliffs and beach. He is attentive and kind, patient and concerned. It is windy. The sea is rough and grey. There are storms coming, but it matters little. For a brief time, I forget everything. Gabriel distracts me with stories about the local coastline, about smuggling and mermaids. I discover he loves the ocean as much as me, declaring the sound of the sea his favourite in the world, along with the sound of heavy rain on the windows. It is cold for the time of year, but we still kick off our shoes and let the sand sink between our toes. We run in and out of the shallows like little children, scouring the shore, picking up sea glass and limpet shells which have been washed in by the tide before heading back to the house.

Back inside we eat fresh pasta with pesto and parmesan before settling in front of the TV under a blanket. We watch old Hammer Horror movies into the early hours with heavy red wine. The muffled numbness still fills my head, but in that moment, we feel like a real couple cuddled up on the sofa. I would not want to be anywhere else but here. I know this will end. He has been really clear in that he does not do relationships, and I have no idea where I will be then. It doesn't matter. I still wish I could pause and save the moment for us. At this point, I do not have the strength to think beyond it.

"You should get some rest," he murmurs. "It's late."

I turn in his arms to look up at him. "Will you come with me?"

He frowns, narrowing his eyes a little and looks momentarily sad. "I'm not tired, and I need to check my emails."

I press my lips to his and the colour rushes to his cheeks. He had not anticipated that.

"I didn't mean to sleep." My boldness surprises me, but I want to be with him. I need to continue to forget the events surrounding me.

"You should rest, Emily. You're still in shock." His voice is low and husky.

"No, Gabriel, I need to feel something. I need to feel you." I press my lips to his once more, sliding my hands around his neck into his hair.

Cautiously, he responds this time, gently circling my tongue with his. I can taste the wine in his mouth. We continue to kiss slowly as the heat and tension rises between us. He scoops me up in his arms as if I weigh nothing, then deposits me gently on his bed, lying down beside me and pulling the covers over us. Clawing at his t-shirt, I can feel the taut muscles on his abdomen, and I graze my hand across his chest and around his back as he pulls his shirt off. I undo my blouse and push it off my shoulders. He unhooks my bra and massages my breasts until they feel plump and heavy. Kissing me again, he explores my mouth with his tongue and strokes my back. I press my body against his and run my fingers through his hair, sliding my hands down his back under his belt into his jeans as I wriggle out of my own. I want him badly. Pulling back and looking at me, he smiles as if I am the most precious thing on earth. He caresses the skin on my inner thighs and between my legs, stroking my clitoris through the fabric of my knickers.

"Please, Gabriel. I need you inside me."

He frowns slightly and hesitates.

"Please, Gabriel. I need you to make love to me."

His frown deepens, and I awkwardly know I have used the L word without thinking. I press my lips to his once more. He smiles in response, sliding out of his jeans and kissing me harder and deeper. I wrap my legs around him, and he moves on top of me, entering me slowly. We move in a lazy, measured dance rhythm. Our bodies glide together as we get lost under the covers in our own little world.

CHAPTER EIGHTEEN

I wake the next morning, and he is still asleep in bed next to me. This has not happened before. His lips are slightly ajar. He looks younger in his sleep somehow and utterly beautiful. His breathing is soft and even, his chest gently rising and falling. It is light outside, but a thick fog hangs in the air. The sea is angry and dark. It is impossible to tell what time of day it is, but it feels late. My watch confirms it is late morning, nearly noon. Apart from the weather it is a perfect moment, and one in which I can momentarily ignore any outside noise mumbling in my head. I remember how attentive and caring he was yesterday. The way he made me feel cherished, protected, and loved. I try to push the feelings away, but I know I am falling hopelessly in love with him.

His eyes flicker open. In this light, there is more green in them than I have noticed before. He frowns, and the mood quickly changes. "Did I sleep here?" There is an edge in his voice.

I smile. "Yes. It's your bed, Gabriel."

He sits up, running his hands roughly through his hair. He glances at his watch, scowling. "Did I say anything?"

I half laugh. "No, not at all that I heard, and you don't snore."

My smile fades as my eyes find his. His expression is ice cold and not welcoming in the slightest.

"I'm going for a run."

He does not look at me, swinging out of bed, leaving me wondering what just happened and what went wrong. I try not to dwell on it, heading to the shower instead and getting dressed. I really need to decide what to do next or at least start thinking about it. My life is my own again, but I have no idea where I am going or the direction I should take. I phone the hospital. My mother is stable and still refusing to speak to me. I know that is the end of it. Nothing will sway her once she has made up her mind. I feel sad. Sad, but strangely relieved, which I try not to over think. Paper. I need paper to scope out my options and plan. It is what I do when I need to make a decision, to give myself a sense of organisation and reassurance.

I am not reliant on Gabriel, however I feel about him and whatever happens between us, which I am acutely aware is likely to be nothing. All that aside, I am thankful I have met him. These past few days have given me the space to start to find myself again and regain the confidence I've lost. In his study, I open the desk drawer. I stop dead. There is a gun. A handgun, like the ones you see in the movies. I have no idea what type, but it looks horribly real. I freeze.

"Were you looking for something?" His voice rings around the room. It is devastatingly cold like the Arctic wind.

"Paper."

"Next drawer." His tone does not soften. "It's not mine, if that's any consolation. It's my sister's, but she wanted me to have it for protection. I didn't have the energy to argue with her."

"Why? Why would you need protection?" This is a whole different world.

He locks his eyes on mine like a target. "Our father has many enemies. My sister is paranoid."

"Do you know how to use it?" I am not sure why I ask, but somehow it would feel better if he did not.

He nods. "Yes, I do."

I swallow hard. "Have you used it?"

He shakes his head. "No, I have not."

There is silence between us, wide and deep. It is like a ravine I am about to fall into headfirst.

He speaks again, outstretching his hand towards me. "Come here."

I go to him hesitantly, unsure what is going to happen next. His mood still feels brooding and unwelcoming.

He pulls me into his arms. "I'm sorry you saw it. It's really not important. You have enough stress in your own life at the moment without me adding to it. Let's get something to eat."

I sit on a stool in the kitchen, watching him make coffee. There is a strange tension between us. I stare at the man I desperately want to be with but wonder again if I really know at all. Tears prick my eyes, and I hate the fact I'm such an emotional wreck.

He turns to face me. He looks earnest. "I'm sorry for being so blunt and being such a dick about it."

I shake my head. "I shouldn't have looked in your desk."

He smiles. His dazzling, hypnotic smile, but his eyes are still wary. "It shouldn't have mattered. Look, I have to work later and first thing tomorrow morning, but let's do something nice tomorrow afternoon?"

My face falls a little. "I can't. I have plans tomorrow."

"Oh? Since when?" He raises an eyebrow curiously.

I know he knows. "I need to go help clear my mother's house."

The storm fills his eyes once more, and his hands hit the counter in a fist, which makes me jump. "Christ, Emily, are you that fucking weak? Why would you help that odious reptile of a brother and your mother? I mean I know she's ill, but from the little you've said she's not much better than he is. It's no wonder they walk all over you. You may as well lie down on the floor and let them do it properly."

I look down, turning my body away from him. He is right, but his harshness shocks me. *Don't cry, Emily,* I think to myself. *Don't cry. You know you are stronger than that.*

His phone is on the counter, and it beeps twice. He sighs as he looks at it and throws it back onto the counter. His mood seems to darken further.

"I think we both could use a little space, and I need to go into the club. I'll see you later. Help yourself to whatever."

He says nothing else. He shoves his phone in his pocket and slams out of the front door. No conversation or explanation. I stand there staring in shock. I am utterly alone and feel like I am in someone else's life. The reality hits me like a truck. I am. I am completely in someone else's life with no idea where my own life is anymore. I slump back down in my seat, staring out the window. The sea thrashes into the shore in squalling waves.

Several hours later it is evening, and Gabriel is not back. The rain lashes against the window. Spurred on by my frustration at myself and anger at his unexplained coldness, I have written several life plans ranging from the obvious go back and finish my master's degree to the more radical look at voluntary service overseas. I have skipped food and am on my second glass of wine. The time goes by surprisingly quickly. By ten-o-clock I am beyond a little drunk and decide to go to bed. I am unsure whether I would realistically want to see Gabriel now anyway, doubting I would be able to articulate my perspective properly in another confrontation with him.

I have not actually slept in the bed designated to me yet and find it incredibly comfortable and soft. The linen is crisp and fresh. I drift into sleep to the sound of the waves crashing with increasing ferocity against the cliffs underneath the house, but my sleep is restless. I awake to the sound of a scream, a scream which cuts through the silence, tormented and agonised. Only semi-awake, I open my eyes. The room is dark. The moon is full, casting dark shadows across the room through the windows. I click on my phone. It is three in the morning. I hear it again, a tortured scream, and I know it is Gabriel. No dream. I am suddenly awake and stumbling down the corridor.

The kitchen is empty and pitch black, except for the moon. I slow as I reach his room. What if he is not alone? I remember the gun and his seeming need of protection. The door is ajar, and I push it open slowly. He is asleep on the bed. The same shards of light from the moon cascade onto his bed and his sleeping form, which tosses restlessly under the covers. The outside columns of light are not on, which is unusual. They seem to be on some sort of timer, illuminating as soon as the sun goes down.

"No-No-Please, no more." His voice is strained and staccato. He sounds scared. He sounds like I have never heard him before.

I move closer to the bed placing my hand on his shoulder. His shirt is wet. It is drenched in sweat, and he is cold, so cold. I whisper his name, and he jerks away violently in his sleep. His breathing is hoarse and rasping.

"Gabriel." I reach for him again.

He shakes in seeming terror, babbling in words that make no sense to me. I fumble for the switch on the bedside lamp and reach for his face. His eyes flicker open. He looks petrified and wild, like a hunted animal. His breathing is so erratic it sounds painful.

"Gabriel, it's Emily. You're having a nightmare. You need to breathe."

He calms, but only slightly, shrugging my hand away and blushing red. He is embarrassed. He continues to shake, and I can see how cold he is from the bumps on his arms.

"Gabriel, you need to change your shirt. You're cold, and it's really wet."

His blush deepens, and I move to his closet, realising I have no idea how he organises his things. Everything is neatly arranged. I find a fawn jumper like the one he lent to me and take it back to him. He hurriedly changes, avoiding eye contact. His breathing is still panicked and labouring. He cannot even look at me.

"Would you rather I left you alone?" I have no idea what to do. I'm acutely aware I am standing over him.

He shakes his head "No, I don't want that." His voice is unusually small.

I sit tentatively on the edge of the bed. "Can I get you a drink or something?"

He frowns a little, nodding in agreement. "Something strong."

I had been thinking sweet tea, but I do not argue with him. I pour him a large brandy in the kitchen and push it into his hands. He is still shaking and sits up with his shoulders hunched. His face is pale and haunted. He looks fragile and vulnerable, two words I never would have imagined using to describe him until this moment. He downs most of the contents of the glass.

"Do you get nightmares and panic attacks a lot?" I decide if I can get him to talk about it, he may relax and calm a little.

"Sometimes. It's better than it was." His voice is hesitant.

"Do you know what triggers them?"

He half laughs, but there is no joy in it. "Oh, yeah, I know what the triggers are."

There is silence between us once more.

"You got an email or a voicemail?" I eventually venture. Was the message the trigger? His mood certainly deteriorated further afterwards.

He glances up at me. Surprised, I think. "I had both. An

email from my father and a text message from my sister telling me to read it."

"Has something happened to your family?" I hear the slight panic in my voice. If it has, maybe that would explain what is going on.

He shakes his head. "No, my father is the chairman of a new charity. He wants me to attend a fundraiser the weekend after next."

This was not the answer I had expected. "What's the charity?"

"It's a charity to help teenagers who have suffered abuse at home and can't stay there." There is no emotion or expression in his voice. It is as if he has shut down.

"That sounds like a good cause." Well, it did. Did it not?

He laughs again empty and sardonic. His breathing races once more. "Yes, a very good cause."

Silence again. The tension surrounding us is almost touchable and increasingly claustrophobic.

"I don't understand, Gabriel." I really do not. "You don't have to explain. I just want to help you."

"I know." He hesitates. "I just don't have the words. It's not something we discuss. None of us do."

CHAPTER NINETEEN

We sit in silence again. He drinks the remaining brandy, leaving me to wonder what is swirling around in his head. His mood is dark and brooding. Whatever it is, it is hurting him deeply. I get the feeling it has probably been hurting him for some time.

Without warning he pushes the sleeve of his jumper up and points to a jagged scar on his forearm. It is long and slightly raised, stretching haphazardly from his elbow to his wrist. I had not noticed it until now. The line is narrow and white, almost like a spider's web on his tanned skin.

"When I was nine, I was playing hockey at school. My family always has. My father displays all the trophies. It's a big thing. Our hockey sticks are custom made. It's the school my father attended, and his father and his father. I let the winning goal in. Fell and sprained my wrist." He pauses.

I have no idea where this going. I wonder why he is telling me about an old school sports injury.

He rubs his fingers over the scar distractedly, as he starts to explain. "My father did not speak on the way home. I knew he was furious. When we got back, he asked to look at my wrist and told me to lay my arm on the table as if he was going to examine it. I knew what was coming, and it did. He slammed the hockey stick across my arm five times in total. He broke my arm in three places. It had to be pinned."

He does not look at me. His voice is flat and strangely detached. We sit in silence as I process what he has just said. He lifts his shirt and points to another scar. It is long and thin, running across his lower abdomen. Again, it is barely noticeable until he points it out.

"He disciplined us regularly. The boys, anyway. Said it was to ensure we grew up to be men who were worthy enough to carry his name. We all had our own belt, but this was when we were on holiday. He forgot mine so he just used the one he was wearing. It had a thick brass buckle which cut into me." He pauses again.

My head is reeling. I feel slightly nauseous. This is probably the last thing I would have expected him to say, but I sense somehow, he needs to tell me.

"How old were you when it started?" I ask hesitantly, not sure if I should ask anything at all.

He does not respond straight away. When he eventually does, his voice is completely emotionless. "When I was five. It was my fifth birthday. My grandparents gave me a train, and I was running it up and down the hallway. He asked me to stop, and I didn't. He threw me up against the wall and stamped on the train. I fell down the stairs and ended up in hospital unconscious for a week or so."

It seems unbelievable, though you read about it in the newspapers often enough. I try to hide my horror. "How did no one know? Where was your mother?"

He shrugs dismissively. "When you have money, a lot of money, people pretend not to see things. My mother was mainly high or drunk. He beat her, too, but not my sisters."

I remembered the photographs I had seen of his mother when I Googled him. She was devastatingly beautiful. You would never have imagined anything was less than perfect in her life until her suicide several years ago There were no hints of abuse in the stories I had read. I desperately want to reach him, to soothe him and make it better. It feels like he is miles away at the moment.

"Did your siblings and you not try to help each other?

You're one of the youngest, aren't you?" I finally venture.

"You imagine we might have bonded together over this?" He smiles faintly, devoid of happiness and empty. "No, he beat all of the boys. I am the youngest. The others would distract him from them to me whenever they could. You're an easy target as the youngest. My brother, Isaac, wrote a letter apologising a few years ago, but I don't blame him. I would have done the same. It's basic survival."

From what I know about Gabriel, I doubted that somehow. Probably best not to go there. "You don't see any of them?"

He shakes his head. "I don't like to, really. It just reminds me and takes me back there. I have some contact with Isaac. I've put him through rehab a couple of times, and my younger sister, Eliza. I don't have any contact with Daniel. He lives off the grid in South America somewhere. I loathe William and everything he stands for. He's just like my father, as is my sister, Jemima."

He stops abruptly. He seems deep in thought, looking down at the bed, his brows furrowed. Silence surrounds us once more. The sea and the wind sound like they are raging a tempest outside. It seems to echo the turmoil, clearly visible in his head.

His voice startles me when he continues. "Actually, that's not fair. I don't loathe Jemima. We've had a better relationship in the last couple of years, hence the gun. You see, it wasn't just the physical stuff with my father. He controlled everything, every aspect of our lives, and still tries to. It's a game to him, and we are commodities. He controlled where we went to school, university, what we studied, who we were friends with, what business deals we initially accepted. His punishments were varied and inventive for rebellion or under achievement. When we were children his favourite was a cupboard in our house in the basement. Dark and damp. The longest I did in there was three days, but Isaac did four. We are both scared of the dark even now, which is pathetic. More than that, though, when I say he controlled everything. I mean everything."

His voice trails off. He frowns, sighing like he wants to say something but hesitates. I stretch my hand out over his, trying to pull him back from the demons which are attempting to consume him.

He pulls his hand away out of my reach before I can stop him, like he needs the detachment. "It was the day before my sixteenth birthday. My father took me to this town house in a nice part of London. It looked ordinary, nothing out of place, but it was a brothel with women he described as disposable. It smelt of sex, and smoke, and whiskey. He took me to this room, and there was this girl there, Lily. Not too much older than me. She was quite pretty in the semi light, but up close she had potted skin caked in foundation and bad teeth. I know now she was probably on meth or crack. It's funny what you remember. She was dressed in this really short skirt and tank top with sparkly red shoes. She joked they were her Dorothy shoes. I was desperately in love with a girl called Tamsin in my year at school. She had no time for me, but I was besotted with her. She was all I could think about as Lily went down on me, then climbed on top and fucked me. You'd think it would be every teenage boy's dream, but I couldn't come. It was nasty. She felt nasty. She was really loose inside, and it hurt. She said I had really good stamina, which pleased my father."

He does not look at me, staring at the bed like he is reporting on someone else's life.

"She told him?" I whisper. This whole story is horrifying. I watch the frown deepen on his face.

He sighs. "He was there. Said he didn't trust us to deliver or the girls not to lie. He was obsessed with us being men. Being dominant. His brother, my uncle, is gay. My father

115

despises him. Says it's the ultimate weakness. I knew I had to perform. Not performing was not an option. Isaac is only two years older than me, and he couldn't get it up. My father fucked him across a table with an empty bottle. He said if Isaac was going to act like a pussy, he would treat him like one. He made me watch so I was clear what would happen if I did the same."

I have no idea what to say. I mean, what could you possibly say? What could you say that would be of any comfort or would make it okay? My head is still trying to put the pieces together and make sense of it all. He continues anyway before I can string my words together.

He is shaking again, his breathing rapid once more. "I thought that would be it, but it wasn't. He took me and my older brothers back to the same house a few times. My father is a violent sadist,

as is my eldest brother, William. The things I saw them do. The fear they inflicted. The degradation. The things they wanted me to do—"

He breaks off, abruptly. His breathing reaches violent levels again, and I can feel him visibly descending back into his nightmare. I reach for his hand, winding my fingers around his. This time he does not pull away. His hands are trembling. He glances up at me, and he looks terrified. Completely tormented.

"It's okay, Gabriel. Don't go there. You don't need to go there."

He calms slightly, but his expression and demeanour are utterly defeated. "I'm sorry. I don't know why I'm telling you any of this. I never tell anybody. I made that mistake once."

His voice trails off, and I know immediately it will be the girlfriend. My dislike of this unknown women deepens. She appears to have really screwed him over.

"You don't need to apologise. Maybe you need to talk

about it. Let it go." Does he need to talk about it anymore? I worry guiltily, maybe my curiosity is why I am willing him to continue.

"Let it go." He repeats my words with no emotion.

His voice is quiet and low. I feel him slipping away again. He starts to pull his hand back away from mine. I catch it before he is able to, pulling it back to me. "Don't go. Tell your father you have other commitments."

He snorts. "It sounds easy, doesn't it?"

The silence opens up between us again like a chasm.

"Is it not?"

He shrugs. "Last time I defied my father, he bankrupted one of my businesses and destroyed my relationship with my girlfriend. As his parting shot, he banned me from my mother's funeral."

"He banned you from your mother's funeral?" My head is in free fall. I remember the fallout from the funeral in the newspaper articles I had read, but it came across that he just did not turn up and did not care. There had been lots of speculation about a family feud and an argument between Gabriel and his mother.

"Yes, though that's not how the press covered it, if you Googled me." He meets my eyes with his which are bloodshot, and I know he knows I did. "I found her. I think she wanted it to be me who found her."

"When she died?" I keep my voice hushed, as if any noise will break him completely.

"Yes, when she killed herself." He looks down again.

"Why would she do that to you?" I hear the despair in my own voice. Maybe there had been some fall out between them, but a mother surely should never do this to her child.

He shrugs once more. "I don't know. A few reasons, maybe. I'd been traveling in Italy for a couple of months, and she'd begged me not to go or to take her with me, but I didn't.

My head was a mess. I wasn't getting on with my girlfriend at the time, and I didn't want the confrontation with my father. I should have known something was wrong. It's not as if her mental health was any secret. It was the day I got back. She planned it that way. I think she worried what would happen if one of the others found her. She wanted everyone to know she had killed herself, not have it covered up, though it was anyway. My father has powerful allies in the press. They made it sound accidental. Like it was a serene event. It was anything but. She wasn't laid on the bed like some Hollywood starlet. She was lying in a pool of vomit covered in bruises from a fight with my father a few days before, but it's her eyes I remember the most, staring up at me like they were looking through me. Dead doe eyes. They will always be looking at me."

I squeeze his hand gently. He stares at the window. I know he can see her. She is looking at him and haunting him. I want to wrap my arms around him, but I worry this will just make him shut down and pull away even more.

He frowns, looking at the bed again. His pain is plain to see, stark and raw. "I was not allowed to attend the funeral. The papers reported some sort of fall-out between us that never happened. People just came to their own conclusions about what a complete bastard I was and still am. Not that I care. I care little what people think, but it hurt me at that time. My father's security made sure I couldn't get anyway near, though one of my father's longest serving bodyguards did let me go to the grave much later after everyone had left. I did say goodbye. I will never understand why he went against my father's orders, but I will always be grateful for it. I've known Mitch since I was a kid. Guess he must have felt sorry for me."

"Maybe he's just a reasonable human being," I counter.

He shrugs dismissively. "Maybe."

"Your father remarried a few months later?" Again, I remembered this from the internet, and he knows already I have looked him up. I wondered where the girlfriend factored into all of this.

"Yes, he did." His tone changes again. It is eerily cold.

"And your girlfriend?" I venture. "You don't need to tell me."

"But you're curious?" His tone is vaguely amused but not in a good way. "Curious to know more about why I'm so fucked up and have such a commitment phobia."

"You're not fucked up, Gabriel."

He is not fucked up from my perspective, though maybe he has a commitment phobia, given all he has said. I sense the conversation is coming to an end and hate the fact my brain still really wants to know about the girlfriend. I suppose it is inevitable.

To my surprise, he continues. "He married her." His voice is devastatingly devoid of any emotion at all.

My mouth drops open. "Your girlfriend?" I whisper.

He nods. "Yes, my stepmother is my ex-girlfriend, only she wasn't my girlfriend. She was my fiancé. No one in my family even knew we were together. We got engaged in secret. I knew my father would not approve. She is a good few years older than me and was not from our circles and was not his choice. I have always been promised to Serena's family. Of course, he knew anyway. I know that now. He had us all under surveillance and still does to some extent. It's partly why I live so far from civilisation. They had been having an affair for a few weeks before I went to Italy. We hadn't been getting on and were supposed to be going together with friends to get some head space, but she made excuses about needing to look after a sick relative I had never heard of and encouraged me to go anyway. I get why now. I think she hoped I would get bored and find someone else to make it easier, but I couldn't have been more in love with her, despite everything. I would have done anything for her. They got married six months after my mother's death on what would have been her birthday."

His voice is unsteady again and has lost the coldness. I sense him descending back to his demons. "He did me a favour really, though it took me a long time to see it. She wasn't who I thought she was. It seems she'd always had her eyes on the bigger prize. I was just a means to an end. I spent a long time afterwards getting drunk and high, fucking any women who crossed my path. Anything to block the pain. Anything to prove to them she meant nothing. That my mother meant nothing. That I was invincible and immune to anything they could do to try to hurt me. A lot of the pictures of me on the internet are from those times. Ironically, it was Isaac who straightened me out with Eliza, though she never knew what had happened in detail. Isaac always says he can recognise the symptoms of self-destruction."

He is shaking again now. It occurs to me he has not mentioned his stepmother by name. It reinforces just how painful and bad this period of his life was, if I needed any confirmation. I just want to hold him, but he still feels too fragile, like he might shatter into pieces. I have no idea how to help him. How to reach him.

"Have you replied?" My words echo around us, as if I am shouting.

The question catches him off guard, and he looks confused. "No."

"Reply now." It is the only thing I can think of to close this down for him.

He glances at his watch. "It's four in the morning, Emily."

I reach for his laptop. "I know, and you're often working at this time, so it doesn't really matter does it?"

He does not argue. I flip open the laptop and hit the power

button to bring it to life. *Password.* I turn the screen to him, and he presses his thumb to it which unlocks it. He pushes it back towards me like he wants nothing to do with it. The applications cascade onto the screen. I click on emails, scrolling down to yesterday afternoon and trying not to pay any attention to the emails before it. There are two from someone called Samantha unopened. Both are marked private and confidential. I think better than to ask. Most of them look like business. The email is simply titled *Fundraiser.* If it was not signed off with *Your father*, I would never have guessed. It is blunt, cold, and authoritative. No frills or civilities and a clear instruction to attend. I shudder as I read the line *You can bring a companion as long as it is not the type of whore who usually accompanies you.*

"What would you reply?" I try to keep any emotion from my voice.

He is frozen. Unmoving. "Just okay, I guess. It's not as if I really have an option."

I type *okay* in the reply. His signature automatically fills in at the end of the email, and I add he will be bringing a friend. I turn the screen back to him to check before I press send.

He frowns, and I explain. "Let me go with you, if you want, as a friend."

He shakes his head, incredulously. "Why would you want to do that?"

"I'm guessing you normally endure these events on your own or with someone who barely knows you, and these encounters leave you in a complete mess. I want to do something to help, the way you've helped me. If you'd like, I will gladly go with you," I reply plainly.

Again, he does not argue. His expression is unreadable. He looks exhausted and desolate. His eyes are still wide, dark, and sad.

I press send before he can say anything else and put the laptop on the table by the bed. "Gabriel, you need to sleep."

"I won't." He sounds convinced, shaking once more. He

needs to rest.

"Yes, you will," I insist.

He continues to shake his head, bringing his arm up around himself like it might comfort him somehow.

"Look at me." I am surprised by the authority in my voice, but he does what I ask. His eyes are glassy and vacant as if he is not focusing on anything. It's as if he is not there at all. He is beginning to really worry me.

"Do you trust me?"

He frowns, and I wonder what he is thinking. Then he nods. "Yes." His voice is barely a whisper.

"Okay, so, lie down for me."

He does what I ask, still frowning. I pull the covers up over him, moving to open and fold back the glass doors onto the balcony from his room. The wind is still raging as the rain beats down relentlessly, but the roof over the balcony shields the room from the water. I feel the chill immediately enter. The sound of the sea crashes ferociously beneath us. It is much louder now. The wind howls in the eaves, but I remember he had said these were some of his favourite sounds. It is nearly dawn. The light is beginning to return to the sky. I turn off the bedside light and climb into bed behind him. He does not move, but tenses as I wrap my arms around him. I know this is what he needs to chase the demons away. To feel loved. To feel safe. This is what he needs.

I pull him back into me and wrap my legs around his. He is cold, really cold. I want to tell him how much I love him, because I do. I know it is stupid, but it's how I feel in spite of myself. I am falling hopelessly in love with him, however foolish that may be. Telling him now will just push him further away. Instead, I hold him tightly, hoping he will feel my love pour into him and soothe him somehow. He is still tense. His body is utterly rigid. I do not let go. Instead I wrap one hand around his waist, the other stroking his hair. Eventually, his breathing steadies, and his cheek drops against my arm. It is wet, and I know he has been crying, silent and alone. He is once again a scared little boy, beaten and locked in a cupboard.

CHAPTER TWENTY

I wake up a few hours later. My arm is still around him, but he has rolled onto his back. Outside, it is still raining heavily. The sea is angry and grey. The room is cold, though it is warm under the covers. I glance at my watch. It is nine-thirty in the morning. He is sound asleep. He still looks tired, but his breathing is steady. Some of the warmth has returned to his skin.

I slide out of bed, and he barely stirs. Knowing he has meetings this morning, I pick up his mobile. He has several alerts and has already missed five calls. I reluctantly press his finger against the screen to unlock it and ring his office from his phone.

"Mr. Hunter-Law?" His PA's voice queries, clipped and professional. "Gabriel?"

"No, my name is Emily, Emily Black. I just wanted to let you know Gabriel will not be coming in this morning." I sound hesitant and unsure.

There is a pause at the other end of the line. "Is everything okay, Miss Black?"

Her tone is one of concern, and her voice is younger than I expected somehow, quietly husky. I wonder if she has slept with him, try to push the thought to one side.

"Yes, he is just unwell and asleep. I don't want to wake him." His relationship with his PA is none of my business. I try desperately to keep my own tone formal and business like.

"Oh, okay." She sounds surprised, and I guess this probably never happens. "Tell him I will clear his diary, so no reason to come in later, even if he is feeling better."

"Okay, thank you."

I hang up and call for a taxi for myself. My bags are packed by the front door. It is ten-thirty when I go back to him. He is still sound asleep. I really do not want to disturb him but know I must.

I gently place my hand on his arm. "Gabriel."

His eyes flicker open. He frowns, looking around. To begin with he looks disorientated, like he has no recollection of what happened, but then blushes red as the memory clearly comes back to him and the shutters crash down around him.

"I rang your PA to say you wouldn't be in today. She has cleared your diary."

He frowns and looks stunned as he meets my gaze coolly. "Okay, thanks. Are you going somewhere?" He looks me up and down with slight curiosity.

"My mother's house," I reply quickly, wondering why he is making me so nervous.

For the first time the conversation is strained, and we observe each other like relative strangers. People who barely know each other.

He nods knowingly, his voice quiet. "Yes, of course."

"To get my things, that's all." I add.

"It's your choice. Don't do that for me. I was a dick. A complete bastard with what I said to you. It's really nothing to do with me. It's none of my business." The cold edge has returned to his voice.

I try to ignore his indifference. "Yes, you were. You were, and your delivery was harsh, but you were right. Anyway, I'm not doing it for you. I'm doing it for me."

He smiles faintly, and the ice thaws a little. "I'll pick you up later if you like."

I pause, knowing I need to face the inevitable. "No, it's okay. I am going to stay with Lucy while I figure out what to do."

The frown returns and deepens. "You don't need to do that. I want you to stay here."

"We could both use some space. So much has happened these past few days, and my head is spinning. I need to work out what to do next with my life."

He is positively scowling now. "You could make a tidy sum selling my story."

I am horrified. Does he really think I would do that to him? The look on his face tells me clearly he thinks it is a distinct possibility.

"I would never do that or do anything to hurt you." I do not know how, but I know this is what his girlfriend said to him as he freezes. "Seriously, Gabriel, I really care about you."

He winces, and it confirms this is exactly what she said to him. I am losing him. He is slipping away. It is plain to see. His expression is increasingly bleak, as he looks away from me.

"Look at me."

He reluctantly does what I ask. There is no emotion in his expression whatsoever now.

I continue anyway. "I wouldn't do that to you because I love you. I'm falling in love with you." My voice rings out and echoes around the room. The words fall like pins on the ground.

He looks blank at first, but as my words register, he looks completely horrified. "No. No, Emily, you can't love me. You mustn't love me. I'm not the man for you. I can't be. I'm fucked up, and I'm cold. More than that, the things I told you last night. The things I've done. You're falling in love with what you think is me, but it's not. I'm not a good person. I am damaged, and I am broken. I don't think I'm even capable of having a meaningful relationship with anyone. You deserve so much more. So much better. I can't give you what you need. I can't be what you need."

I raise my finger to his lips to silence him. I do not want to hear anymore. I know I need to be strong, although part of me is dying inside. He stares at me with a lost, bewildered look in his eyes.

I run my hand through his hair and across his face for one last time. "I know it's not what you want. I get it. Love's a two-sided dream, but you can't change it. Neither can I. It's how I feel. I just wanted you to know."

Before he can respond, I kiss him gently on the forehead and leave. I step outside the front door without looking back, pull the door closed behind me, and stand in the pouring rain.

CHAPTER TWENTY-ONE

The taxi has not arrived yet. I know I cannot go back inside. Instead I stand there like a statue, letting the rain lash down on me. Finally, inside the cab, I am wet through and frozen. I am aware my mascara will have run down my face, so I must look like a cross between Alice Cooper and a demonic circus clown. My hair clings to my face like coils of wet, fraying rope. I know Gabriel will not come after me, though a little part of me hopes I am wrong.

"You all right, flower?" The taxi driver glances at me in the rear-view mirror, confirming I must look an absolute state.

He is an older man with a big grey beard and broad Westcountry accent. His face is kind. I just nod, and he pulls away, not speaking again.

The rain is still pouring down as I knock on Lucy's door.

Rob answers. His initial expression of distraction is quickly replaced by one of concern. "Bloody hell, Em?"

He ushers me inside and through to the lounge, wrapping a towel from the laundry basket in the hall around my shoulders. Lucy is playing with her son, Noah, on the rug. She gets up as soon as she sees the state of me and sits beside me on the sofa. I cannot speak, feeling awkward and embarrassed. I know if I try, I will just cry and genuinely worry I will not be able to stop.

"I'll make some tea." Rob disappears into the kitchen, and we sit in silence until Lucy cannot bear it any longer.

"What the hell did he do? Did you argue? Did he hurt you?" There is clear anger in her voice.

I shake my head, and Rob returns with the tea. It is overly sweet, but warm and soothing. Everyone is silent except Noah, who continues to drive his truck around the floor, utterly oblivious, which I am thankful for.

"Hey, Noah." Rob's voice surprises me. His tone is light and bright, as the little boy looks up. "Shall we go and surprise Nanny and see if she has any ice cream in her freezer?"

Noah nods eagerly, and they are gone.

Everything comes pouring out. Lucy sits quietly as I pour out my heart without interruption. I omit the graphic details of Gabriel's nightmares. The rest comes flooding out, like the water currently falling from the sky.

"It's my fault. He was very clear he doesn't do relationships from the start," I conclude, my voice strange and raspy.

When I have finished, Lucy takes my hand. "No, honey, it's not your fault." She hugs me as the tears continue to roll down my face.

I cry to the point it hurts and I cannot cry anymore. I text him later and stare at the blank screen for about an hour debating what to send. I settle for a completely unimaginative, *Hope you're okay x*. I wonder if the kiss is too much. He knows how I feel now anyway, so it does not really make any difference. I sit over analysing to the point of obsession. He does not reply. I knew he would not.

The next week rolls by slowly as I stumble through it. Everywhere I go I am reminded of him. From the coffee shop, to carnations in the shop, to pictures of him in the gossip columns and society pages. I feel wretched. The ache in my heart is insurmountable. I do not sleep, and when I do it is restless. I cannot eat, and I feel like I am descending lower and lower into oblivion. He is haunting me. He is the first thing I think about as I open my eyes and the last thing when I finally go to sleep. Even a trip to the beach with Noah reminds me. I can see his house in the distance, which I had never even noticed before. His silence is deafening, and my defeat becomes deeper rooted as every day passes. I was a fool to ever imagine anything would or could come from this, an idiot to give my heart so easily, but it matters not. I am his completely.

The police contact me to let me know they are dropping their investigation in relation to David and my mother being financially or physically abused or neglected. They do not go into detail except to say there is not enough evidence, and my mother is not being cooperative. I know this means I am unlikely to have any contact with her again. I feel strangely relieved in some ways, which just makes me feel guilty, but I also worry for her. I write two letters to her via David's address, to let her know I am thinking of her and am here for her in the hope she receives them but am under little illusion that she will.

It is Thursday morning again, and I am unpacking a flower delivery for a funeral on Friday. Lucy slams her magazine shut as I walk into the back room and attempts to hide it under the counter. She avoids eye contact.

I raise an eyebrow. "That good? What was it?"

She shakes her head. "Nothing, just the usual nonsense."

She is lying, and I just know it is something about him. I narrow my eyes and outstretch my hand. She hands me the magazine sheepishly. It is a weekly gossip glossy, and the front cover indicates there is a whole page inside about Gabriel and a mystery woman. I would never have previously taken any notice, other than maybe to have subconsciously acknowledged him as a ridiculously attractive, nameless man. The picture is of him stumbling out of a nightclub with a stunning blonde attached to him like a limpet. She is wearing a short red jumpsuit which leaves little to the imagination, while he looks stunning as he always does, in black jeans and a black shirt which is only buttoned up halfway. His eyes are hidden by sunglasses.

I scrutinise the picture, hoping it is a throwback from the times we discussed, but quickly see it is a new club which opened at the weekend. I turn the page quickly, and a lump forms in my throat. What did I expect? I mean what did I honestly expect?

"It doesn't mean anything." Lucy ventures.

I shake my head, fighting hard to hold back the tears, my voice strained. "It's not really a surprise is it? I mean that's his reputation after all."

"You should ring him. Seriously. He cares about you. The way he was with you at the hospital. The way you talk about your time together. I can't believe that's all there is."

I shake my head. "No, there's nothing more. It was great. He was great, but I wonder if I really knew him at all. Maybe it was just an act. The way he dazzles and draws people in. I don't mean deliberately, but I'm not sure I saw the real Gabriel. It's certainly not the Gabriel who appears to be seen everywhere else. The Gabriel everyone else knows."

Lucy looks thoughtful. "Maybe that's the point. Maybe he doesn't let most people close enough to get to know who he really is. Sometimes it's easier to hide if you let people believe you're what they already think you are."

I shrug, returning to my work on the funeral flowers, not particularly wanting to think about it. Maybe she is right. Maybe he *is* the quietly shy thoughtful man I saw glimpses of repeatedly, but he seems to try so desperately to keep hidden. Maybe that's not him at all, and he is the celebrity lothario, the media enjoy reporting on so much.

We remain in silence for the rest of the morning, except when I need instructions. I retreat into myself. The shop bell rings, and Lucy goes to greet whoever it is. We currently have an unspoken agreement I am better not dealing with customers. I do not bother to look up as she returns. Instead, I focus my attention on stabbing a lily with floristry wire.

"Um, I think these are for you."

I look up and see she is holding a huge bouquet of purple, red, and white roses with pink carnations, tied with black ribbon. Each bloom is perfect. The scent is intoxicating even from this distance.

I shake my head. "No one would buy me flowers, especially ones like that."

She grins. "I can think of one person. The delivery guy definitely said your name, and it's your name on the card. Please tell him the next time he feels like spending this much money on flowers to call me. Thoughtful, too. White roses for purity and innocence. Red for passion and desire. Purple for enchantment and love at first sight. Not sure where the carnations fit in. They're just a little odd."

"They would be for The Jam if they were from him and he cared much about the meaning of flowers, but they won't be from him." I am certain of it.

She raises an eyebrow, thrusting the flowers into my arms. "Really, and The Jam? Well, only one way to find out."

I recognise his writing instantly. My hands tremble. What is this? Goodbye flowers or apology flowers, maybe? He was very clear he does not do sentiment or romantic gestures, despite the glimpses I saw. Either way I do not have any confidence this will be anything positive, however beautiful they are. I pull the card from the envelope.

I am so sorry, Emily. Please call me. Gabriel

I feel confused, overwhelmed, like a wave has just gone over my head and dragged me under to the depths of the seabed.

"Emily?" Lucy pulls me back to the shore. "Everything okay?"

She looks concerned, but then she has been the one stopping me from drowning this past week and trying to piece me back together.

"He wants me to call him."

"So, call him."

I feel annoyed suddenly. "What, so he can give me some excuses and get it off his chest, then say goodbye and feel like he was nice about it and that we are friends? I don't want to talk to him."

I am lying. We both know it, but I worry the sound of his voice alone will tear me into two again.

Lucy pushes my phone towards me. "Of course, you want to talk to him."

I sigh, defeated, and pick up the phone. It rings twice. A woman's voice answers, and I freeze.

"Hello?" the voice asks for the second time.

"I was trying to reach Gabriel." My voice is shaking. Is this the woman from the photo?

"Is that Emily?" the voice queries.

"Yes," I murmur.

"Oh, Miss Black. It's Gloria, Gabriel's PA. We spoke last week. He's in meetings. His phone is on divert, and he's not taking calls, but I am to put you straight through if you ring. Hold the line please."

I hear a ring tone and a voice, his voice. "Hello." His tone is clipped and harsh and does not sound like him at all, which throws me. "Hello?" the voice queries again.

"It's Emily." I am immediately annoyed at myself for not being more assertive.

He exhales sharply. "Excuse me, gentlemen, I need to take this call."

I hear him walking and what sounds like a door and the sound of the ocean. I assume he is at the club.

"Emily." He sounds almost breathless now and like my Gabriel. "I wasn't sure if you would ring. Did you get the flowers?"

"Yes." My thoughts and words have left me. "They're

beautiful. Thank you."

He pauses, and I wonder what he is going to say. I feel dizzy, almost winded and disappointed in myself for letting him make me feel this way with just a few words.

"I wondered if you had plans for this weekend and if you would still come to the fundraiser with me, like you said. It's fine if you can't. I would completely understand if you don't want to." He sounds hesitant, to my surprise, almost nervous.

"Can your new friend not make it?" It is a childish, cheap shot, but I have to ask.

"My new friend?" He sounds confused, then it clicks. "Oh, right. Are you asking if I fucked her, Emily?"

His directness surprises me. I have no clever retort despite all the things I had planned in my imagination. The silence grows between us until he continues.

"For what it's worth, I didn't. I fully intended to fuck her, but when it came to it, I don't know. It just didn't feel right. Everything felt wrong. She was really pissed off. I'm sorry you saw the photos." He sounds measured and calm. "I get it if you don't want to come on Saturday."

I feel like an idiot. My head is spinning. Why did it not feel right? I push the thoughts to one side. This really is nothing to do with me, though my heart feels slightly lighter momentarily. His breath echoes in my ear, along with the sound of the sea lapping gently in the distance.

"No, it's fine. Of course, I will." I do not hesitate. I had already agreed to go. Do I really want this? Probably not. I know I am just setting myself up to get hurt even more, but I also know I cannot resist seeing him again, in any circumstance. "I said I would, and I meant it."

"Great." His relief is obvious. "We need to leave about four. I was thinking maybe you'd like to spend the day at the club. At the spa. I could get my personal shopper to pick out some dresses for you to look at and choose from."

This annoys me. Is he suggesting I would wear something inappropriate? "I have my own clothes, Gabriel."

He sighs and sounds edgy again. "Hey, yeah I know. I just thought it would be nice. You know, kind of fun. I thought Lucy could come with you."

I can hear I have hurt his feelings. It occurs to me that maybe he was just being nice. The suggestion made with the best of intentions. In reality, I have nothing to wear to such an event, and my bank account is not in a mood to oblige a purchase of evening wear.

I concede. "Okay, that would be lovely." I hate the awkwardness between us. It is like we are both tiptoeing around each other.

I hear him exhale. "Great. I will ask Gloria to put a schedule together and send it over."

Silence again, just the waves crashing in the distance.

"I'll see you on Saturday, Emily." His voice is husky now.

It ignites the dormant desire and aching passion in me. Urgh. This is going to be more difficult than I initially thought. I am only attending as his friend.

"Yes, I will see you then." In two long days.

"Emily . . ." his voice breaks off.

"Yes, Gabriel?"

"It doesn't matter. I will see you on Saturday." He sounds reticent and regretful once more.

"Okay." I wonder what he was going to say. Guess I will never know.

"I miss you." His voice is crystal clear and utterly genuine.

The line goes dead as he ends the call before I have the chance to respond.

CHAPTER TWENTY-TWO

The schedule arrives thirty minutes after I have put the phone down. It is accompanied with an instruction to say we can change whatever we like on the day. It looks amazing. Personal shopper and dress fitting. Followed by massages and facials. Break for lunch, then manicures, pedicures, makeup, and hair. Lucy is beside herself with excitement at the prospect of all these treats. I, on the other hand, am wondering why I am doing this. I would willingly walk across hot coals for this man but am also painfully aware I am leaving myself open and vulnerable again. Like a moth flying directly into a naked flame.

Saturday takes an eternity to come. We stand in the foyer of the main Incubus building just before nine in the morning. The shiny black stone floor gleams in the sunshine, as the sleek and silent glass doors open and close. It is surprisingly busy.

Lucy moans about how early it is and how she is usually never up at this time. "Who are we actually waiting for?" she queries quietly.

"Not sure," I reply, which is true enough.

The schedule simply said to be here for nine in the morning. I glance at my watch. One minute to go. That is when I see him. Wearing a dark indigo blue suit with a fresh white shirt, he strides across the foyer like a panther. His whole look is crisp and expensive, as he ignores the stares of all the people around him. He trains his eyes on me like a sniper, but his expression gives nothing away. My legs turn to jelly.

"Emily." His eyes do not leave mine, as if I am the only person in the room, all-consuming and bordering on rude. He remembers himself and nods to Lucy, murmuring good morning. His tone is cold and formal, like it had been on the phone.

I begin to regret agreeing to this. My heart is heavy and aching at the mere sight of him. This feels like a formal arrangement. Friendship, at the very best. I did not need to reopen this wound—a wound which has not even begun to heal yet. I start to feel stupid and out of my depth once more. We are a million worlds apart. As we follow him to the lift, Lucy raises an eyebrow.

The lift moves slowly to the seventh floor. The small restricted space seems to enclose around us. He looks forward stoically, but his presence is suffocating. The tension crackles around us so you can almost touch it.

"Is it getting hot in here?" Lucy chuckles.

She can feel it, too. I glare at her, and she looks away, still smiling.

The lift pings and stops. He exhales deeply as if he has been holding his breath, steps out of the cab, and strides forwards. The empty space outside his office has been transformed into a dressing room with mirrors and rails of clothing. I admit to being completely intimidated by the thought of a personal shopper. I am sure it will feel awkward and patronising, but the women I am confronted with puts me at ease. She is older, with kind and gentle blue eyes. I would guess mid-fifties, dressed in fitted black trousers and an immaculate cream blouse. Her light brown hair is coiffured into an elegant bun.

Gabriel kisses her formally on both cheeks. "This is Bridget. She will help you to choose an outfit for this evening, unless you decide to wear something else." His tone remains business like, as if he is making arrangements at a meeting.

I note he has not forgotten my comment about having my

own clothes and is being careful. The heat rushes to my cheeks anyway while I shuffle awkwardly on the spot.

"I'll pick you up from the restaurant bar downstairs at four." He nods at Bridget, who simply smiles. "Excuse me. I must go, but I need to borrow Emily briefly first." He strides back towards the lift.

I follow cautiously, not sure if this is what he has intended. He turns abruptly. He is so close I can smell him, sandalwood and limes.

He cups my face gently in his hand, still frowning. "You look tired, Emily."

I do not respond. He stares into my eyes as if he is searching my soul. What am I supposed to say? *I have not really slept since I left your house and have spent most of my time being in tears or over-analysing our time together?* He, too, looks less than rested.

"I hurt you, and I'm sorry. Deeply sorry. I never meant to. I really didn't, but that doesn't make it any better." His voice is deep and earnest. He sounds sad, his hand still warm against my cheek.

I shake my head, "I let you hurt me. You were really honest with me from the start."

He sighs, still frowning. "It didn't give me the right to hurt you. I should have got in touch with you sooner."

"Why didn't you?"

He is making no sense to me at all, and I feel my resolve crumbling.

His frown deepens. "What you said. It scared me."

"Scared you?" My confusion deepens. I could understand indifference or annoyance, anger even, but scared?

He wraps his hand around my waist as he tilts my head upwards, pulling me into him. His body is hard as stone. He presses his lips to mine with a voracious hunger, greedily invading my mouth with his tongue. Longing for his touch and his closeness, I reciprocate eagerly. I have missed him. Really missed him. He tastes of coffee, rich and strong. My body moulds into his. I stretch my arms around his back and cling to him like he is my rescue and salvation. Pulling apart, we are both breathless and flushed. I am aware Bridget and Lucy are watching from the other side of the room, but I am beyond caring. Nothing else matters in this moment.

"Because of how it made me feel," he replies huskily, releasing his grip on me so the space grows between our bodies. He does not allow me to question him further. "I have to go to a meeting. I'll see you later."

As he leaves, I walk back to Bridget and Lucy, a little unsteadily, slightly embarrassed, and confused.

"Just friends, right?" Lucy exclaims. "Sure looks like that. What do you think, Bridget?"

Bridget smiles tightly. "It's really not my place to say."

"Do you do this for Gabriel often?" I query, desperate to change the focus.

Her smile grows more kindly. "I pick out clothes for Mr. Hunter-Law regularly, but this is the first time he has asked me to help a lady friend, which is a most enjoyable change."

My mind spins once more. His words still ring in my ears, and now this. I just assumed this was something he set up regularly, but what does it mean? Maybe this is due to all his other *lady friends* being capable of dressing themselves appropriately. I try to block out my inner sarcastic voice, but it chips away at me anyway. I am drowning slowly.

Bridget interrupts my self-pity. I am not sure if she is aware of what she is doing, or if it is just good timing. "Shall we take a look? Mr. Hunter-Law was very clear on what he thought you may like and colours. I have a good assortment."

Bridget is not exaggerating. So many beautiful dresses with eye watering price tags. It is like something out of an expensive glossy magazine. I do not know where to even begin. I am shocked at how many I immediately love and surprised by Gabriel's attention to detail and Bridget's interpretation of my likes and dislikes. We finally all agree on a long fitted blue dress with vintage lace, which looks almost like clouds in the sky. It has a sweetheart neckline and thin bootlace straps. There is an accompanying long coat in midnight blue velvet, which Bridget explains may be necessary later in the evening if I need to be outside. Bridget accompanies the dress with matching blue high heeled satin shoes, crystal jewellery, clutch bag, and a dark blue lace shrug. She insists I do not need the shrug, but I hate having my arms on display. I look in the mirror and barely recognise myself.

"You look absolutely stunning." Lucy beams.

I feel confident and nervous, both at once.

"I suggest you wear your hair down, but have it pinned at the sides. I have some hair clips which would work perfectly with this outfit," Bridget continues, rummaging in a display box to retrieve two silver clips with what look like pearls and blue glass. "Now let's look at clothes for the rest of the weekend."

"The rest of the weekend?" I query.

Bridget looks confused. "Yes, my dear. You are expected to be away with Mr. Hunter-Law until Monday, I believe. You will need an outfit for the Races, nightwear, and something casual." She gestures to a suitcase I had assumed was simply part of the things she had brought. "I understand Mr. Hunter-Law's housekeeper has packed the toiletries you like, and you will be arranging makeup here later."

This is different. I had no idea we were away for the whole weekend.

Lucy nudges me. "Hmm, like I said, just friends."

My anxiety and excitement rise at the prospect of a weekend with Gabriel. But the Races? I have no idea what is coming or how this is going to be. I do not have time to dwell on it for long. Bridget quickly identifies a bewildering array of items, including a cream dress adorned with flamboyant flowers in red and vivid green leaves for the Races and a black silk nightdress with matching nightgown which reminds me of my seduction of Gabriel in his study. I'm flustered as I see the price tags, though some items do not even have them. That is a lot of money in one suitcase. Bridget explains this will all be packed for me and accompanies us down to the spa.

We are scrubbed and massaged mercilessly with frangipani and other exotic oils in dimmed lighting, followed by facials. I feel utterly relaxed. I do not think my face has ever felt so clean or moisturised. In robes, we are shown to a private booth in the club restaurant which overlooks the main dining area. We can observe the other diners unseen. A waiter appears with a bottle of champagne.

"I could so get used to this." Lucy squeezes my arm.

The restaurant is busy, as is the spa. Looking around, I wonder if Gabriel is still in the building, but if he is, I do not see him. After lunch, we are escorted back to the spa where we are given manicures and pedicures. Makeup is applied and my hair styled in natural waves and the clips Bridget suggested. I look in the mirror and again barely recognise myself. At the same time, it does still look like me, just a very refined, polished version. I wait for the beautician in the reception, and my gaze is drawn to a large painting on the wall. It is the one I noticed when Gabriel showed me around the club and I discovered who he was. It is of the sea crashing into the cliffs on a stormy day. The detail is incredible. You can almost smell the sea. The colours are an array of greys and blues, with hints of green and purple against the white of the spray and sea foam.

"It's good, isn't it?" I have not heard the beautician return behind me.

"Yes, is it by the same artist as the others?" It looks different and I am not sure why I even ask.

She smiles. "No, it's one of the owners."

I am confused. I know Gabriel owns the club and everything in it. "How do you mean?"

She half smiles. "He painted it. Went mad when it turned up here with the others he'd ordered from Cornwall, but we all persuaded him to leave it here. You're his friend, aren't you? Didn't you know he painted?"

She emphasises the word *friend*. I see she is a little intrigued as to what I am to Gabriel, probably like the other people we have met today, but this is the first time anyone has actually said it.

"Yes, I knew he painted," is all I respond. I look in the bottom corner and see his initials confirming what she has just said. I would never have guessed. I understand now why Judith is frustrated he no longer paints.

I find myself reunited with Lucy and Bridget, who dress me in my evening outfit. I feel nervous once more, not so much of Gabriel, but the whole situation and what I am about to walk into.

"You look gorgeous, Em." Lucy is staring at me. "There's no way he's going to be able to resist you looking like this. Don't you agree, Bridge?"

Bridget smiles, but winces slightly, I think at the shortening of her name. "The colour and cut certainly suit and flatter you, Miss Black."

We thank her and head down to the bar.

CHAPTER TWENTY-THREE

The restaurant is surprisingly busy, considering the time. All the booths are taken, and people stand in most of the available space. We sit at the bar. It is a little before four in the afternoon. I start to feel nauseous and slightly ridiculous, since I am the only one there in full evening dress. Lucy sits so she is looking directly at the entrance. I look forward into the bar, counting the many bottles as my nerves consume me. She nudges me, and I know it means she has seen him. I turn as he strides across the bar towards us. He seems oblivious as always to the many eyes following him.

He stops less than a metre in front of me in silence. Smiling, he runs his gaze over me, from head to toe. "You look stunning." His smile reaches his eyes and lights up his whole face

I feel the colour flush to my face. "Thank you." I feel shy and coy somehow. "So do you."

He is wearing a black tuxedo with a bow tie and immaculate white shirt. He looks even more gorgeous than usual, like James Bond.

He continues to stare at me, then remembers himself, widening his view to include Lucy. "Did you both have a nice day?"

I do not manage more than a nod.

Lucy has no such problems. "Yes, it was great, thank you. I'm going to try and use some of the hair and makeup tips for my wedding."

He frowns a little. "It's in a few weeks, isn't it?"

Lucy nods. "Yes, three now."

He smiles. "Come in, and we will get everything sorted for you."

"It's been lovely but no. Our budget . . ." Lucy babbles regretfully.

He cuts her off. "Please, and no budget. It will be on us. I assume you have bridesmaids, mother of the bride, and all of that?"

Lucy looks unusually dumbfounded. "Um, yeah mums and two bridesmaids. Emily is my maid of honour, but seriously, that's too much."

His smile widens. "That settles it. You will all come here, mothers included, and yes, you can. You've been a really good friend to Emily, and this is just a way to say thank you."

Lucy beams, and my heart warms. "Gosh, that's lovely of you and very generous. Thanks. I don't know what to say."

"It's nothing. I will get all the details from Emily and set something up." He turns to me now. "Emily, remind me, if I get distracted this weekend."

Distracted? The way he says it is utterly sensual and suggestive. I feel myself swoon on the spot.

"Please excuse us now though, or we're going to be late." He holds his arm out, which he clearly means for me to take.

He watches with vague amusement as I just stare at him. I turn to Lucy and hug her.

"Go get him," she whispers in my ear.

I cringe before taking his arm, sure he probably heard her. He immediately sweeps me closer into him. His body is warm and firm. He smells divine with the usual notes of sandalwood and lime I will always associate with him. We walk through the bar, and I am aware of the many eyes watching us, but it does not matter to me anymore. Outside, Guy is waiting with the black Audi. He smiles when he sees us and moves to open the passenger door. Gabriel gets in the other side. Despite the small distance between us, I still feel the allure and pull of him like a magnet. He turns to look at me.

His expression is soft but unreadable. "We will get there in about an hour and a half. I'm really sorry, but I have to take a conference call." He rolls his eyes. "Unfortunately, a lot of my business associates will be at the event, so nowhere to hide. It does mean you'll have my full attention for the rest of the weekend."

"No problem." It makes no difference to me, and it at least gives me time to get my head together. "Where are we actually going?"

He frowns. Yet again I have agreed to go somewhere with him with no idea where that actually is.

"Oh, it's at my grandfather's house, my father's parents in Somerset." His voice is calm, distinctly controlled, and pragmatic.

The sense of familiarity is between us like before. At the same time, things feel formal and slightly uneasy. I know he is being cautious and holding back, but from what, and why? I try to ignore it. I agreed to do this. Willingly offered, in fact. Still, it does not stop me wanting to feel his body on mine or his arms around me. The arousal and my desire for him threatens to consume me. There is also of course the kiss—the kiss from earlier, and his statement that what I said had scared him. I have no idea what to make of either. My brain is free-falling through too many emotions.

His laptop is open, and his phone rings. His voice is clipped and devastatingly cold again as he talks about shares, I think, and some sort of investment. He does not notice me looking at him. It is as if he is not really sitting there within touching distance from me. He looks really tired. Beautiful and undeniably hot, but tired. His eyes are still haunted. I wonder if he has had more nightmares and panic attacks, but also how he deals with them on his own. I suspect he does not deal with them and either drinks them away or just does not sleep. Has this always been there? I wonder if I only notice it now that he has told me and I am looking for it. I know I look tired. I doubt, though, he has been a sobbing wreck like me, despairing at himself in a tide of self-pity.

He catches me looking at him and smiles gently while telling whoever is on the other end of the line to *get a fucking grip, for heaven's sake.*

There it is, the two sides of Gabriel side by side, perfectly juxtapositioned. I am sure there are many more facets to him. I have no idea which ones are truly him and whether I will ever know. I spend most of the rest of the journey staring out of the window while half-listening to his conversation. I am fairly clueless as to what he is talking about. The thoughts swirl around in my head like boats set adrift in the tide with no anchor or final destination.

Within the hour, we pull off the motorway onto a B road through the Somerset countryside. A little while later we drive onto a narrow road across a country estate until we pull up outside what looks like a stately home. The grounds we have just driven through belong to it. Then it dawns on me. This is his Grandparent's house.

"This is it?" The amazement in my voice is all too apparent, although I attempt to disguise it.

"Yes, this is it," he answers plainly as he steps out of the car.

Guy opens the door once more. Gabriel is there with his hand outstretched. Several other cars pull up, and he leads me inside.

The house is as impressive on the inside as it looked from the outside. A huge staircase cascades down into the main entrance hall with plush burgundy carpet on to the entrance floor, which is black and white chequered tiles. The walls are wood panelled with large opulent oil paintings hanging in ornate wooden frames. I feel like I have walked into a heritage site or National Trust property, not someone's home.

"You okay?" he half-whispers.

"Do they actually live here?" I query softly.

He smiles softly. "Yes. Well, they did until recently. They've moved into a smaller property in the west wing of the estate. Downsized, my grandfather would call it. The main house is open to visitors now at certain times in the year and for functions like this one."

"Will they be here tonight?"

"I doubt it, highly." His tone is unreadable.

"Do you see much of them?" I want to ask if he gets on with them but feel the need to tread carefully.

His smile remains, which I take as a good indication. "Yes, a bit. Not that often, but I quite like their company if I ignore their link to my father. My Grandfather may be at the races. He likes the odd flutter. My Grandmother's not well and pretty much bed bound, so I don't tend to see her. She's a very proud lady and would rather we didn't see her like she is now. We do write to each other occasionally. Very old fashioned, but she really likes to receive a letter."

I wonder about his relationship with them and how it works if they know about his father. Maybe they do not know, but that would seem unlikely.

He seems to read my mind. "They're very proper. Very English. They're not the sort of people to dwell on problems and would prefer to turn a blind eye. Stiff upper lip and all that. It used to piss me off, but I kind of get it now. They only ever saw glimpses, not the full deal. They would be horrified, but they would also struggle to believe it. As long as you accept those rules and can play that game, they are entertaining enough. My Grandfather has taught me a lot, ironically."

"Gabriel!" A shrill, excitable female voice interrupts him. A dark-haired woman in a pea green lace dress with a long string of double pearls, which looks like something a 1920s flapper would wear, throws herself around him with enthusiasm. "I wasn't sure if you would come."

As she pulls back, I can see the family resemblance.

He smiles a warm, genuine smile. "Of course, I was going to come, Eliza," he chides.

Her large brown eyes observe me curiously, her focus falling to observe my hand in his. "Who is this, Gabe?"

"This is Emily, Eliza."

"Who is Emily, Gabe?"

I know what she is getting at, but he ignores her, instead turning to me.

"Emily, this is my younger sister, Eliza."

"And his older brother, Isaac. Hello, brother," a low male voice adds behind us.

We turn to look at the man standing there. Again, there is an obvious family resemblance. His features are not as defined as Gabriel's, and his overall appearance is slightly dishevelled. He, too, embraces Gabriel, who responds accordingly, rubbing his brother's back. I admit to being vaguely surprised. I had not expected him to be so warmly greeted, from what he had said about his family. I do recall him saying he was in touch with Eliza and Isaac, though, remembering he had put Isaac in rehab.

"We haven't seen you in like forever, Gabe." Eliza pouts at him.

"Indeed, little brother. You have been even more elusive than usual lately, but perhaps now we can see why," Isaac half-scolds, observing me shrewdly.

Gabriel shrugs, a little flustered. "Busy with work and the club. Emily, this is my brother, Isaac."

"Very nice to meet you, Emily." Isaac smiles. He has Gabriel's smile, though his is more crooked.

With his siblings still eying me curiously, Gabriel seems keen to move them away from their current conversation. "What's the format for tonight, and who's here?"

Isaac's demeanour changes immediately.

Eliza answers for both of them. "Oh, you know, the usual hangers on from the society pages and Father's business associates. Jemima is here somewhere. As is William. Father will not be here until later. I think Jem said seven-thirty. Dinner is at eight, and the auction is part of that. Some of the items are on display upstairs, unless you just want to bid on wine. You and Emily are sitting with us for dinner, so plenty of time to get to know each other better." Her grin widens.

Gabriel rolls his eyes. "Great. Well, I guess we'd better go look at auction items and mingle. See you guys later." He sounds less than enthusiastic.

"Later, big brother," I hear Eliza chirp as we start to walk up the staircase.

Gabriel is greeted by numerous people who either ignore me or stare at me curiously. His body language generally tells me at best he tolerates the majority and loathes quite a few. His outward manner remains polite and coldly cordial. We do not encounter his other siblings. I debate whether he has deliberately dodged them, because they must know he is here. Everywhere we go people are staring at him and me, whispering in groups. I wonder why he is creating quite so much attention. It occurs to me perhaps this links back to the time his mother died and reports of a family feud.

He does not comment on it, but he cannot be oblivious to it. We acquire a drink each from one of the many waitresses dancing around the guests with silver trays, champagne for me and what looks like brandy for him. We circle the lots for the auction. Gabriel explains the items have been donated and many will not be on display, like trips abroad, vintage wine, or bucket list experiences. The things which are on display include bespoke glass ornaments, a large hamper of exotic delicacies in exquisite packaging, designer luggage, and beautiful handmade jewellery. I presume the jewellery is made with diamonds, accompanied by other jewels like sapphires and emeralds, judging from the reserve prices.

"Pretty, yes?" he queries.

"Yes, beautiful. It's absolutely stunning." I do not think I have ever seen jewellery quite so beautiful.

"I know the designer. We went to school together. She uses the sea and the elements as her inspiration like cobwebs or the rain. See?" He points at two pieces, and I nod. He sighs and seems bored. "Would you like to get away for a little bit and have a tour of the house?"

"If there's time." I agree it would be good to escape while we can.

He nods. "Yes, a good hour or so. I'm already tired of small talk and pleasantries."

I follow him through the house away from the gathering crowd. It is as exquisite as I thought it would be. Every room we walk through is adorned with more beautiful paintings and extravagant furnishings. He explains the history of several of the paintings, including generations of ancient ancestors and landscapes. I quickly get the impression they are all originals. In a large dining room we walk through, a glossy wood table fills the room with seating for at least twenty people. It is so shiny and immaculately polished it looks almost like glass.

I walk a little way in front of him into the next room with a large mirrored wooden dressing table and lots of coats. It is quite dark. Green velvet drapes shield the window. I see it is some sort of cloakroom and turn to walk back out, assuming he had not meant to lead us into here. As I do, his body crashes into mine. He kisses me with an intensity which takes my breath away. We slam against the door devouring each other hungrily. His body is tight against mine, and I want him, really want him. He locks the door behind me as he presses his lips to mine.

CHAPTER TWENTY-FOUR

He continues to explore my mouth with his tongue mercilessly. His hands are firm and strong as he presses them against my body. He moves his mouth down to kiss my neck.

"Stop, Gabriel, please stop." My breathing is fast and unsteady.

He stops and pulls away instantly, frowning. He finds my eyes with his. His gaze is earnest and searching. My eyes focus on him as he penetrates me with the intensity of his stare.

"I'm sorry. I've missed you. Really missed you. I wanted to show you how much I've missed you. It was rude and presumptuous of me to imagine you feel the same way."

The irony is I do want this as much as he does, it would seem. I want him here and now as if it will claim him somehow and reconnect us.

"I do. I've really missed you, too."

His frown deepens. "Then what's wrong?"

"We'll be missed, and I'm worried about ruining my dress." This is half true.

He smiles mischievously, as he continues to stare into my eyes. "No one will miss us. This is just the arrival and mingling stage. As for your dress, I was going to help you out of it." He runs his hands down my back.

It is not only my dress. How can I tell him *I am scared of getting hurt*, or *I have been breaking my heart all of last week*, or *I am fragile and vulnerable, and I do not want to go back there?*

"What are we doing?" I hope he might somehow understand the depth of what I mean in these few words.

I expect him to say something sarcastic or suggestive, but he does not. Momentarily, he looks unsettled, I think understanding my meaning.

He leans forward resting his forehead on mine. His eyes are closed. "I don't know. I really don't know."

I circle my hands around his back under his jacket and pull him fully back into me, pressing my lips to his. I can't help it. I want him, irrespective of the likely fallout for my heart. I want him, and I need him to know I want him. His response is immediate. He roams his hands over my body, behind me, finding the zip on my dress. I shudder as he strokes my bare skin. The electricity and excitement build between us. He steps back and lowers the dress from my shoulders. I step out of it, watching as he hangs it carefully on the back of a chair, before turning back to me.

"Fuck, Emily. What the hell are you trying to do to me?" He runs his eyes over me approvingly.

I remember the lingerie I am wearing. Balconette bra and side tying knickers in midnight blue silk and lace with stockings and suspenders. Leading me away from the door to stand in front of the dressing table, he watches me expectantly. He finds my mouth with his once more, kissing me deep and strong and lifting me so I am sitting on the table. I stretch my legs out around him, feeling the bulge in his trousers rub against me. Desperate to touch his skin, I pull his shirt from his trousers and unbutton it with clumsy fingers. He unties his bowtie, leaving it loose around his neck. I run my fingers across the muscles on his chest and stomach. I undo his belt, pulling him back into me, impatient to feel the friction between my legs. The excitement of doing this here and the chance of discovery is both frightening and a complete turn-on. Kissing my neck, he runs his fingers along my bra, pushing the cups down to release my nipples which are already hard and long in anticipation of him. He teases them with his tongue, sending shockwaves down between my thighs. I want him badly.

He returns his eyes to mine, dark and lustful. His cheeks are slightly flushed. Pulling the tie from his neck, he smiles and takes my hands, raises them above my head, and ties them together. Then, he ties them to the bracket under the shelf above the mirror. I shiver as he runs his hands down the length of my outstretched arms, back across my chest and down between my thighs. His fingers are inside my knickers massaging my clitoris. I am utterly exposed and turned on. He smiles kissing me once more, pushing his tongue deep into my mouth while his fingers thrust into me. I am so alert and aroused. The way I am going, I think I may just come in his hands. I know he can feel it.

Dropping to his knees, he pushes my knickers to one side and kisses my clitoris. He rolls his tongue over me while he continues to push into me with his fingers. I am so close. He teases me with his tongue between my legs, cruelly. I want to run my fingers through his hair. The fact I cannot frustrates me and turns me on. I am on the brink of climax as he sucks between my legs. He removes his fingers, pushing my legs further apart, giving him deeper access to me. Having undone the bows at the sides of my knickers, he easily pulls them off and shoves them into his jacket pocket. He pulls back just as I think I am going to lose it, smiling wickedly. His gaze does not leave mine as he stands, undoing his trousers. He does not lower them, but I see his penis escape, fully erect and proud. It seems bigger than I remember. I need him inside me, craving the release.

"Please, Gabriel, now. I need you now."

He smiles, moving between my legs. With one thrust he is inside me, stretching me around him. I pant and tilt my hips to pull him deeper into me, feeling full. Too full. Like the first time once more, as he rolls his hips and grinds into me. He glides his hands under my buttocks, pulling me onto him. I climax quickly, letting go completely, feeling myself throb and clench to a crescendo all around him. As I calm, he is still rock solid inside me. He looks at me almost devilishly. We are far from finished. His penis is still fully erect as he withdraws, now covered in a sheen of moisture from me. Half-smiling in a sensual sexy way, he releases my hands from the hook and unties them. We do not speak. The only sound is my heightened breathing.

Lifting me off the table, he moves us both to the end of the narrow dressing table. He reaches up to the coats behind him and pulls a fur coat down across it. Turning me, he bends me over it, outstretching my arms so I grip the far side. I wonder fleetingly who's coat it is. It smells of expensive florals and musk. The fur tickles my naked breasts, which are escaping my bra. He stands behind me stroking my legs and my back, then fists one of his hands into my hair. His other hand works beneath me to find my nipple, which he pinches. With long strokes of his fingers, between my thighs, he makes me even wetter and lustful.

As I look into the mirror, my gaze finds his. His expression is dark and unreadable, but utterly sexual. He pulls on my nipple once more. The fur tickles the naked flesh of my inner thighs. His hands move behind me and push my legs apart once more until I stand astride. He pushes me forward. My bottom is in the air, naked except for the suspenders and stockings. I watch him watching me and taking in the view, deliberately making me wait. He is standing so close behind me his erection presses against my bottom through his trousers while he massages my buttocks.

Without warning he slaps the right cheek, making me yelp with surprise. He massages the same spot. The blood rushing to my flesh sensitises me. He pauses now, watching my reaction, waiting for me to confirm I want him to continue. I simply nod. I watch a smile flit across his face as he repeats the action with the other side. Firm slaps, then sensual massage. The massage chases away the sting and makes everything between my legs clench as I squirm beneath him.

"Stay still," he instructs. His voice is low and husky as he repeats his sweet torture with both sides once more.

It feels wrong but so right. The fact I am watching him in the mirror makes it even more erotic and forbidden. Everything between my legs throbs relentlessly. I arch my back and find myself waiting impatiently for his palm to flatten against my skin again. It does several times more until I am wound up like a spring. He continues to lock his gaze on mine in the mirror. His expression is carnal and brooding. I can feel the heat in my buttocks.

My nipples rub against the softness of the fur. He enters me, hard and unyielding. Pulling my hips up with his hands, he pummels into me, rocking me against the table. His eyes do not leave mine as I arch my back further and he cups my breasts in his hands. He thrusts into me relentlessly with a rhythm I cannot match. I can feel him moving deep inside me as my vagina pulsates and tenses around him. The fur tickles my clitoris and between my legs while he thrusts deeper. I hear myself scream his name. I am without abandon and completely oblivious to where we are as he comes. I throb around him, milking him and taking everything he is offering. He leans forward, holding me and kissing my neck gently. His bare chest falls against my back as the aftershocks move through us and his erection ebbs away.

"Are you okay?" His voice is a sensual whisper.

I nod, unable to speak. His embrace around me tightens. Safe and warm. This is what I wanted. Apparently, it is what we both needed. Any awkwardness and tension between us before dissipated. We lie in a tangle of limbs in our own little bubble for what feels like a long time, until he brings us back to reality.

"We need to get back to the party." His voice is heavy with regret as he stands and buttons his shirt. "There's a little bathroom through the side door, if you need to freshen up. I'll help you back into your dress."

I stand awkwardly, turning to face him and retrieving my knickers from his pocket. Reaching my arms up around his neck, I knit my fingers in his hair. I kiss him deeply and slowly. The colour rushes to his cheeks once more, and he looks shocked. I smile. I have no idea what I am doing or where this is going, but I figure I may as well enjoy it. I am sick of over-analysing every conversation and exchange we have.

Looking in the bathroom mirror, I feel relieved. The reality of where we are and what we have just done begins to sink in. Incredibly, my makeup is completely intact, and my hair still sleek and styled. I fasten my knickers and apply some lipstick and perfume from the handbag Bridget picked out for me. I feel a little less confident as I walk back into the cloakroom in my underwear. He is fully dressed once more, leaning up against the door and drinking the brandy he brought with him. He smiles and offers me the glass. My nerves evaporate as he helps me back into my dress.

"Whose coat was that?" The fur is still draped over the dressing table, and I feel guilty about it.

He laughs. "No idea. Guess that will teach them to wear fur."

"That's quite an alternative anti-fur campaign," I counter.

He laughs once more. We both laugh. He takes my hand, leading me back into the dining room. His hand is warm, and I feel like we are connected by some invisible force. We are about to walk back into the auction room when a voice stops us.

"Gabriel."

His whole-body tenses beside me. His jaw is tight, and his posture adversarial. The voice comes from a woman in a striking red dress. Her long dark hair cascades down her back in soft waves. She is wearing a large diamond necklace with drop earrings. They look real. She is stunning, and I wonder who she is. With her is a man who looks like an older version of Gabriel, but without the softness. His features are harder, with eyes grey and dead like a shark's. Gabriel looks straight forward as if he is frozen to the spot.

"Gabriel, your father is arriving shortly. You should be downstairs." Her voice implies he is in trouble. It occurs to me she is speaking to him like a child, though she does not appear to be much older than him.

"Which is where we're going." His voice is ice cold and edgy. "Emily, this is my stepmother, Samantha, and my brother, William."

Oh, hell. Now I understand why the climate has just reverted to the ice age. Samantha looks at me curiously, as does William, but his gaze is distinctly critical. After a moment he places his hand on Samantha's arm. He whispers something in her ear which makes her look uncomfortable. Her expression is suddenly distant and sad, and he leaves without acknowledging us further.

"Serena is here, Gabriel. She said she had not seen you." The implication in Samantha's statement is crystal clear.

He simply shrugs with the unspoken message he could not care less on loudspeaker.

She sighs, continuing anyway. "You look tired, Gabriel."

"What of it? I have a lot of work on currently." He frowns, and I sense he is losing his patience. "So do you, Sam. Is Father treating you well? I did warn you what you were getting into, but I don't think you ever heard me."

She visibly flinches. "Have you warned Emily, Gabe? She doesn't seem like your usual type."

157

The gloves are off, and the history between them is threatening to bubble to the surface.

He smiles without any warmth. "Cheap shot, even for you. Why do you even care? It's nothing to you. We should all be going downstairs. I don't suppose Father will be any easier on you than me if you keep him waiting."

She flinches once more, reaching out and touching his arm. He jerks violently away from her. His attempt at cold indifference is immediately shattered in pieces all around us.

"Do not touch me." His tone is quietly furious.

"Gabriel, please." Her voice almost pleads. "I need to talk to you. I've left you messages. Emailed you. I need your help. It's very rare I see you when no one else is around."

I assume I do not count as someone else.

Gabriel's frown develops into a full scowl. "We have nothing left to say to one another. We ran out of words a long time ago. I can't help you even if I wanted to."

We all stand there as if no one can move until William returns and takes Samantha's arm. I wonder what she wanted to talk to Gabriel about. I want to dislike her, and I do for what she has done to him. At the same, I cannot help but feel a little sorry for her.

"Are you okay?" I whisper as they walk away from us. I search for his eyes with mine. When I find them, they are surprisingly warm.

He squeezes my hand. "Yes, I'm feeling pretty bulletproof right now. Thanks to you. Though my attitude maybe a little dangerous in our present company. Come on, we need to go downstairs to dinner."

CHAPTER TWENTY-FIVE

W e do not see Gabriel's father as we are swept into the main reception with the general tide of attendees. The room is softly lit with large floral displays. Abundant flowers in gilded vases and crystal glasses sparkle under the strings of lights hanging from the ceiling. The tables are exquisitely decorated with linen in cream and gold. We sit at one near the front with Eliza and Isaac, accompanied by two older couples. Eliza sits next to me, ignoring the seating plan and her date. Gabriel whispers to me he is an old friend from school who is actually gay and in a long-term relationship. I see William and Samantha at a table across the room from us with an older man. I assume it is Gabriel's father, but I cannot get a good view of him. I am strangely intrigued by him, like a fly observes the spider's web. At another table, I see Serena and the others from the bar. She pretends not to have seen us, and maybe she has not.

For dinner, we are presented with seven courses starting with a salad of roasted candy stripe and golden beetroot. The meal concludes with locally sourced cheese and port, followed by coffee and petit fours. It is a beautiful and elegant meal, like a fine dining restaurant. I admit to being famished, as it seems is Gabriel. I am also a little tipsy after a different wine is served with every course, along with a champagne.

Eliza interrogates me throughout the meal, but I warm to her and find her constant banter amusing. Gabriel fails to rescue me several times, as does Isaac. She does not directly ask me what Gabriel is to me, but I know she is trying to work it out. He answers a few of the questions she throws at him and ignores others or deflects them by rolling his eyes. It is interesting to see him with his siblings. In this moment, he seems happy and distracted, completely free of the stress and anxiety I had witnessed earlier.

The auction happens through coffee, and all three bid. I assume they are expected to. Gabriel buys one of the glass ornaments, a large bowl of delicate blue green glass for the club, which reminds me of the sea and the one at his house.

After the meal, we all go outside to watch the most spectacular fireworks display I have ever seen. Gabriel stands behind me. He wraps his arms around me, pulling me into him. Still no contact with Serena, though many others want Gabriel's ear. I think it is odd but am pleased at the same time. It is late when we go inside. Gabriel suggests we say our goodbyes so we can escape. It has been a surreal evening and really enjoyable which I dare not dwell on in fear of jinxing it. I was convinced it was going to be a lot harder than it has been. Eliza throws her arms around me and then Gabriel, making him promise we will all meet up again soon. Isaac is more reserved but kisses me gently on both cheeks and whispers to me he is glad to see his brother so happy. I wait for Gabriel as he retrieves my coat.

"Emily."

I do not recognise the voice, which is deep and sharp. Neither do I recognise the man who says my name as I turn around. I know instinctively who it is, though. A much older version of Gabriel with a dark, commanding presence. His eyes appear to look right through me into my soul, cold and piercing.

"You do not know me, and we have not been introduced." My feet take root as he observes me shrewdly. "I am Gabriel's father. Have you seen my son? He has been a little elusive this evening."

I blush. It is as if he knows why Gabriel and I disappeared

earlier and what we were doing. Maybe he does. I feel embarrassed and vulnerable. I wonder how he knows my name or why he would even need to know or care. My memory of Gabriel's description of how he likes to control every aspect of his children's lives floods back to me.

"He's just getting my coat."

I sense Gabriel before I see him. He takes my hand in his, which his father glares at briefly. Gabriel stands silently. His posture is visibly tense, but I can't tell whether he is ready to run or stand and fight. He swallows hard like he is waiting for something.

"There he is. Gabriel." The way his father says his name sounds like singing and emphasises each syllable, but there is no kindness or affection in it. "I was just saying to Emily I have not seen you yet tonight."

"We have been here all evening, Father." Gabriel's voice is flat and emotionless.

"Indeed. Well, there are a couple of things I need to discuss with you." His focus returns back to me. "Did you have a nice evening, Emily?"

Again, he seems to elongate my name as if he is dissecting it. I simply nod.

"Good. I imagine it is different to your normal social engagements. If you would excuse me, I need to talk to my son for a few minutes. I will not keep him long."

I wonder what he means and what he knows about me. My own flight instinct starts to kick in.

Gabriel's hand tightens around mine. "There's nothing you can't say in front of Emily, Father."

His father raises an eyebrow, and the tension around us builds further. A woman with chestnut brown hair and green eyes, wearing a sumptuous black gown, appears next to him.

"Gabriel." Her tone is formal, but warmer.

"Jemima," is all he replies.

The older sister. The evening continues to unravel around us, like some sort of soap opera.

"Is everything okay, Father?" she queries.

He raises a hand to silence her, but her very presence reduces the latent aggression surrounding us a little. "Yes, I have a couple of things to discuss with Gabriel." His focus rests on Gabriel like a target. "I have some business I need you to pick up for Lionel. Investments. He needs to move some money around overseas, without leaving an obvious trail."

Gabriel shudders. He hunches forward scowling, his voice wary. "What business and why not William?"

"You are the best. Far better at the markets than William and far more discreet in your transactions. I know I can trust and rely on you to do it properly." His father sounds genuine in this view, although I am not sure if it is a good thing. "You do not need to know, Gabriel, as I have said many times."

"And I have said many times I will not be involved in things I know nothing about."

His challenge surprises me. I glance at him to see he is maintaining eye contact with his father.

His father laughs hollowly. "Indeed, you have, Gabriel. As you wish. Lionel is establishing an orphanage in Thailand."

I feel Gabriel tense further, his body rigid. "What age?"

"Early teens."

He shakes his head, his mouth set in a grim line. "No, no way."

"You think you can say no?" His father places his hand on Gabriel's upper arm and squeezes hard, making him flinch and look down. "I will arrange for all of the details to be sent to you. Now for the other matter. Your arrangement."

Gabriel frowns, still staring at the floor and looks unsure. "My arrangement?"

"Yes, with Serena."

He looks up again. "Emily knows about it, Father, so you

don't need to talk in riddles. Anyway, what of it?" He sounds weary and exasperated.

His father grins widely like a Cheshire cat. "I misread the situation. Emily, if you are aware, perhaps you are like the girls he normally brings here after all."

"You know nothing about Emily," Gabriel snaps.

His father laughs once more. "Perhaps not, but it matters little. We are intending to announce your engagement next month."

"No, absolutely not. I have never wanted this. I haven't agreed to it, and neither has Serena. I am also not thirty until next year." The anger in Gabriel's voice is clearly evident.

"What difference does a few months make? Besides, Serena is more than happy, which is why you have not spoken to her this evening. She didn't want the embarrassment of being photographed with you on a date with another woman with the announcement pending. A little humiliating, but I have assured her it won't happen again, and I will pull you into line. Again, you don't need to agree to this. I am merely telling you."

Gabriel shakes his head, his tone quietly furious. "No, I won't do this."

"I wonder what has brought about this change. You do remember how I will make you toe the line?" His father is glaring at me once more, his tone cruel.

Gabriel continues to shake his head, the colour rushing to his cheeks. "No change. You know how I feel about this. I've never wanted this."

"I am not interested in how you feel or what you want. This is a business transaction for the family. No emotions necessary. You are not known for having meaningful relationships with women, so what does it matter?"

I want the ground to open up and swallow me and to take Gabriel with me.

"Gabriel, you just need to get your head around it," Jemima interjects, her voice firm. "You knew it would happen. You just weren't expecting it now, darling. That's all."

Gabriel continues to shake his head.

His father smiles nastily now, his mouth twisted into a smirk. "I suggest you get your head around it quickly and end unnecessary attachments. This is going to happen. If you do anything to jeopardise these arrangements, there will be consequences." His father pauses, allowing the threat time to sink in and fully register. He turns to me once more. "It was nice to meet you, my dear."

The tone of his voice makes me shudder, and the fact that he is intimidating me scares me. There is something genuinely chilling in his manner. I watch him walk away, leaving Jemima with us.

"For heaven's sake, Gabriel. You know better than to provoke him," Jemima scolds Gabriel as if she is the parent.

He shrugs like the corresponding petulant child. "I've done caring, Jem. I can't live like this anymore. I won't."

"He knows you are in contact with Samantha."

His hand tenses around mine as he looks directly at her, his eyes blazing with fury. "What are you talking about?

His apparent anger does not appear to have any impact on her.

She smiles calmly in response. "You're saying you are not?"

He shakes his head, indignantly. "No, I'm not. She's emailed me and left a couple of voicemails which I've not listened or replied to."

She looks surprised, then distrustful. "Are you sure?"

"Very. Why is that a surprise to you?"

"Many reasons. You were in love with her, and now you hate her. The two emotions are relatively close. If nothing else, curiosity." She stares at him as if she is analysing his reactions.

He shakes his head again, clearly struggling to keep his temper in check. "No, you're wrong."

"That you loved her? Please, Gabriel. She broke your heart, and we nearly lost you. In fact, I am not sure we ever truly got all of you back."

He laughs coldly, composed once more. "No, that I hate her. I don't. I feel strangely ambivalent towards her. As for curiosity, we all know what happened to that cat. I have no idea why she's contacting me, and I've deleted the messages and the emails unread since last week, so leave it. I don't need you to fight my battles for me, and I don't need babysitting. Do you understand?"

"Hush." She purses her lips. Her voice is strangely soothing and more conciliatory now as she hugs him awkwardly. "Hush, baby brother. You clearly do. Don't do this. Don't do this now. He nearly destroyed you the last time, and he will happily destroy you and everything you care about again. I'll ring you, and we will catch up properly next week. I'll ring Gloria to set it up, okay?"

"Whatever." He sounds exhausted, like he does not have the energy to fight anymore.

I wonder if these encounters always take this much out of him, as we walk towards the door.

A male voice I have not heard before, clipped and cold warns, "Careful, little brother."

We both turn, and I see it is Gabriel's older brother, William. Gabriel does not speak, the scowl clearly etched onto his face

William continues, clearly amused. "Indeed, take care, little brother. We're all on the edge of our seats waiting for you to hit the self-destruct button again. Would you like some help?"

"Go to Hell, William." Gabriel's voice is hushed and low.

I glance up at him. I can feel the anger pouring off him in

waves. He looks utterly furious and in truth a little scary. His eyes are dark, and his expression seriously brooding.

William just laughs, smug and nasty. "I'll save you a seat. We both know it's where we will all end up, no matter how much you think you have distanced and redeemed yourself."

I wonder what he means. Gabriel shakes his head but says nothing further, tightening the grip of his hand around mine and leading us away.

We do not speak on the way to the car or when we see Guy, and we get in. I do not know what to say. He continues to hold my hand in his.

"Do you want to talk about it?" I desperately want to help, to support and soothe him, but he feels unreachable. It is like he has built a high wall around himself to provide distance from everything and everybody.

"No, babe, I'm all out of talking," he whispers.

I feel him shutting down and pulling away with his demons. I cuddle into him, wrapping my arm around his waist. He gently rests his chin on my head, and I listen to his heart beating through his shirt. I am almost asleep by the time we get to the hotel a little while later, shattered despite my attempts and best efforts to stay awake. I yawn as he opens the car door for me.

"Let's get you to bed, sleepy," he murmurs.

"It's fine." I try to protest, but I know it is no good. We are both done.

He leads me through a hotel lobby in semi-darkness. It looks like another stately home. There is an impressive and imposing marble fireplace opposite the reception desk. The reception area is decorated with green walls and dark wood, filled with tall-backed leather armchairs and a large rug which looks like tapestry. He half carries me up a grand wooden staircase and along a corridor into one of the few rooms on the third floor.

CHAPTER TWENTY-SIX

I do not remember getting into bed. The last thing I do remember clearly is him carefully unzipping my dress and taking my shoes off. I am pretty certain he did not come to bed with me, but as I wake the next morning, he is lying beside me. The light streams in through the French doors leading out to what appears to be a balcony. The room looks amazing in the semi light, huge and airy. The bed is ridiculously comfortable, like a giant marshmallow, with sumptuous bed linen in tones of burgundy, grey, and cream. A large bunch of white lilies sits on the table by the door, which I can smell even from here. It is silent other than the birds I hear singing outside.

He is asleep on his back, bare-chested with one arm above his head. His long eyelashes rest on his cheeks. He seems peaceful and rested, like he has fallen from the sky. I watch his chest slowly rise and fall. His hair is gently tousled and messy. He is almost angelic in his sleep. Undeniably gorgeous, but innocent somehow. I touch his chest softly. I am not sure why. It is almost as if I cannot believe this beautiful creature is real and lying here next to me. His skin is warm. I outline the shape of the muscles on his chest and stomach with my finger. He stirs. His eyes flicker open, closing again softly. He opens them again with a flash of warm brown. He glances around looking a little disorientated, until his focus finds me.

"Good morning, Emily," he murmurs.

I wait to see his reaction, remembering the last time he

167

woke up in bed beside me.

He frowns, still not fully awake. "Is everything okay?"

I smile. "Yes, I'm just thinking about how you don't usually seem to like sharing a bed."

He stretches both arms above his head. A smile drifts across his face. "Oh, right. Yes, well, I think you can probably work out why."

"Because of your nightmares?" I confirm, my hand still on his chest.

He pauses. "Yes, but more than that. Sharing a bed is intimate. You are vulnerable when you're asleep. Your guard is down, and there's nowhere to hide. I'm quite shy deep down, though I don't tend to show anyone that side of me very often. I've rarely felt any desire to put myself in that position since Sam, to feel exposed to someone in that way. Hideous morning conversations and awkwardness."

He is being honest and open, which both surprises and pleases me. I am also surprised he mentions Samantha by name and has described himself as shy. The more I think about it, the more I realise he is probably very self-aware. It is true. The real him, the him I think is real, is much more reserved. Away from the spotlight he is creative and quiet. Much less extravagant and exciting than his press coverage would ever suggest. He does not appear to be feeling particularly awkward in this moment. I stroke my hand across his chest once more. He smiles softly, watching me trace the muscles on his stomach with my fingers. I feel bold and in control. I am pleased he has not shut down with me this morning, which I had half expected.

I dip my hands lower on his stomach under the cover, where his erection greets me. "Oh, my, Gabriel. You've only been awake a few minutes."

He looks amused. "I always wake up like this. It's not unusual. Have you not heard of morning glory?"

I shake my head. "No, I've no idea. Seems a shame to waste it, though."

I pull back the covers. He stares at me still smiling, while I reveal the bulge in his boxer shorts.

"Really, Emily, and what are you planning to do about it?"

I pull his shorts down enough to release him, taking his penis in my hands and watching his eyes narrow. His breathing hitches a notch, and I move my fist up and down. Shuffling down the bed, I take him into my mouth. His skin is warm and soft between my lips. He tastes slightly salty.

"Fuck, Emily."

I smile with him still in my mouth, finding his eyes with my own. Circling my tongue around him, I dart it over the tip. I know I have him. In this moment, he is mine completely. Moving to straddle him, I lower myself on top of him, and his penis stretches and fills me. He pulls at my nightdress, stroking my thighs.

I slap his hands away. "No, Mr. Hunter-Law. You can look, but please do not touch."

He smiles, clearly amused and raising his hands in concession. I pin them with my own by his head. We both know he could easily release himself, but he does not, happy to play this game. I move slowly on him, up and down as I find my pace. Losing all inhibition, I really ride him. He continues to stare into my eyes. The colour floods his cheeks, and he turns his head to the side. His breathing grows rapid. He is close. I rub harder up and down on him, forcing him deeper inside me and feeling the warmth travel through my body. My name is on his lips as he comes deep inside me. My own climax builds to its crescendo. I clench around him, continuing to move, until I slow and wind down. Collapsing on my belly beside him, I turn to look at him. His breathing is still heavy.

"Awkward moments like this?" I ask innocently.

He grins, laughing without abandon. "Yes, Emily, just like

this."

Still grinning, he gets off the bed. I watch his naked body walk into the bathroom and I hear the shower. I lie there on the bed, rolling over onto my side, drifting in and out of a contented doze. My clitoris is still swollen and throbbing between my legs. I clench my thighs together to maximise and extend the pleasure of the sensation, trying not to dwell on the return to Devon tomorrow and leaving Gabriel again. I wonder what the day will bring. This morning could not be more perfect so far.

I do not hear him come back in, still deep in my own thoughts. Instead, I feel his hand slap my bare bottom and him lying behind me, wrapping his arms around my waist. He is damp and wearing only a towel. He smells deliciously of lime.

"Emily, my love, you can't lie naked on the bed like this with your delectable ass in the air and expect me not to react."

He purrs as he kisses my neck softly, and his hands reach down between my thighs, his body spooning around me. I arch my back into him, throbbing back into a climax as he strokes my clitoris, which is ready for him. I come easily and lazily in his hands. He moves slowly, but he keeps his hands between my thighs, moving my legs slightly apart and rolling me onto my front. He is inside me once more, the one in control now and thrusting into me. He continues to stroke my clitoris. I climax again, violently, almost painfully, while he comes. His erection fades as he kisses my neck, and he rolls me back onto my side. He wraps his body around mine again from behind, pulling the covers up around us.

"I ran you a bath, I thought you may want one." His voice is deep and suggestive behind me.

"Hmm." I can barely move. "Thank you. Do we need to go soon?"

"No, not for a few hours yet. Are you hungry?"

His voice is so damn sexy. I nod in response. I am too high on sex for a proper conversation.

He laughs. "Okay, I'll get some food sent up. Anything you fancy?"

I turn in his arms to face him, pressing my body to his. He continues to grin at me.

"Hmm." I murmur again, kissing him and running my hands down his back.

He smiles knowingly, wrapping his arms back around me. His naked body is tight against me. He is all I can feel, smell, and see. He presses his lips to mine so I can taste him, and we get lost under the covers once more.

Sometime later I have bathed in luxuriously rose scented water. In fluffy white bathrobes, we have eaten warm croissants with rich fresh coffee, charcuterie, cheese, and fresh fruit. We sit on the balcony in the balmy sunshine overlooking the hotel grounds. Dressed for the races, I go back to the balcony. He is working on his laptop wearing a chocolate brown three-piece suit with a crisp cream shirt. He looks stunning, as always. The tiredness from yesterday has completely gone from his features.

"Do I look okay?" Somehow, I need his approval, as much as I don't want to admit it.

He looks up. His expression is serious, but his face quickly breaks into a smile. "You look beautiful, and I really like your dress. Not sure about the jewellery though."

His comment throws me, and my face falls a little. The only other jewellery I have with me is from last night, and I know it won't work.

He stands and moves towards me. "Yeah, I really don't think it works." He starts to frown and looks displeased.

"Okay." I do not know what to say or understand. Why is this such a big deal?

He half smiles, reaching into his laptop bag and bringing out a glossy wooden jewellery box which he holds out to me. "Maybe something like this would be better. What do you think?"

I open it with trembling hands and see it is the raindrop necklace from the auction last night. It is stunning, but there is no way I can accept it.

"It's beautiful, but I can't accept this. It's too much."

He shakes his head, his expression thoughtful. "Yes, you can, and no, it's not. Anyway, I wanted to say thank you for coming with me last night."

"You don't need to thank me." He really doesn't. Does he not get it? I feel almost offended at the inherent suggestion of being paid off.

"Maybe not, but I wanted to. Here, let me help you put it on."

He fastens the necklace around my neck. His fingers tickle my neck as he fastens the clasp. It makes me shudder. He moves me to a mirror for me to see it. It is truly beautiful. I feel like I might dissolve into tears. I am so happy I think I might burst but also utterly confused. I have no idea what to think or whether I should think at all. He does not need to thank me. I came willingly because I love him. I want to help and support him. Does he not understand this?

It dawns on me I still have no idea how he feels. He was careful not to introduce me as his girlfriend yesterday. There is also his marriage, which I already knew about and now feels like it is pending. I really am a complete fool. The realisation that maybe this is just an enjoyable weekend between two friends with benefits hits me once more. I fight to keep my emotions in check.

"Are you okay?" He finds my eyes with his. He looks concerned and confused.

I had almost forgotten he is standing beside me. I nod,

swallowing hard and trying to dislodge the lump in my throat. He takes my hand, leading me downstairs to the awaiting car and Guy.

Chapter Twenty-seven

As we arrive at the Races, my anxiety rises again. I have even less idea what to expect here than I did last night. Gabriel has been vague about why we are here other than his father expects it, most of the people from last night will be here, and he likes horses. I fidget in my seat. I do not like the unexpected.

Gabriel takes my hand. "You look very beautiful when you are not fidgeting. You'll be fine."

As we walk inside, I am confronted with men in expensive suits, some top hats and tails, and women in beautiful dresses and flamboyant hats. It looks like the footage you see at Ascot. We move through the crowds onto the terrace. Eliza waves at us from afar, and I recognise William and Jemima, who are talking animatedly by the doorway.

"Father. Samantha." Gabriel walks right up to them, which surprises me.

His father also looks vaguely surprised. The tension still crackles between them, but Gabriel seems more in control today. It dawns on me how confronting them now maintains his sense of control and gets it out of the way. Samantha looks down at the floor and away from him.

"Gabriel." The way his father says his name will stay with me. Intimidating and passively aggressive. "Less elusive today, I see. And Emily. Nice to see you again."

Once more, his tone implies it is anything but nice.

"I have some business to attend to. Is Grandfather here?" Gabriel's tone is deceptively bright, but distinctly guarded.

"No, he is not well this morning. Sciatica. We will see you later maybe. If not, heed what I have said, Gabriel. The business details have been sent to you. I will be in touch shortly about the other matter."

We move away from them, and Gabriel's mood noticeably lifts again. We mingle, and Gabriel has several business conversations. I understand how securing agreements out of the boardroom in a less formal setting makes things more relaxed and friendlier. Gabriel blatantly takes advantage of this by making a large donation to the pet charity of one of his business associates to help abandoned dogs. He orders a bottle of champagne, and we move up to a quieter area of the terrace away from the others to watch the preparation and warm up for the races. Gabriel explains the pedigree of some of the horses or shares snippets of information about their owners and trainers, some of whom he knows. He is excitable like a child, warm and charming.

"Gabriel!"

I recognise the voice behind us immediately. Serena. We both turn, and he tenses, looking down at the floor.

"Gabby!" She leans in, kissing him on both cheeks. She looks stunning in a navy-blue dress, her blonde hair shining in the sun like a halo around her. "And with Emily again, I see."

He smiles tightly but does not respond.

"I didn't get chance to see you last night." She implies something else with her tone. "But Father said you are aware the engagement will be announced soon. Not the best time to be seen on a date with someone else, if that's what this is, Gabby?" She looks me up and down, glaring.

"Would you rather I left you alone to have this conversation, Gabriel?" I desperately want to run and hide from Serena glowering at me. I feel thirteen again, being picked on in the school canteen by the popular girls for not having the

175

right pencil case.

Serena answers for him. "Yes, that would probably be best, Emily."

He takes my hand before I can leave. His voice is strained, and I sense angry. "No, Emily, that absolutely will not be necessary."

Serena glares at us both now. "Gabby, this is not appropriate. We are about to be married. Your reputation is bad enough, but you can't go around with another woman now. I know this is different for you, but it's time to put the flirtations and sluts to bed without you, darling. Emily isn't even from our circles or one of the usual disposable one-night stand types you bring to events."

"No, she's not, Serena. Emily certainly is not, and you and I are not going to be married."

She looks confused. "What do you mean? Our fathers have agreed to the arrangements. I have agreed."

"I mean we are not going to be married. I don't love you. You certainly don't love me. I have never agreed to this. You know how I feel about it. I have always been really clear." His voice is dangerously calm and utterly controlled.

She shrugs. "Yes, you've been clear, but what does that matter? What has love got to do with it? You don't believe in love anyway. We're friends. I have been your friend for all of your life, and we're from the same circles."

"We're not friends," he corrects her coldly. "We happen to know each other. Anyway, who says I don't believe in love?"

Her eyes widen a little, and she looks surprised. "Your behaviour and your usual female acquaintances would suggest it, and your own words about love and relationships."

She is right. The conversation I have had with him about relationships is playing on a nearly constant repeat in my head.

"People change," he replies matter-of-factly.

She laughs, looking me up and down. "No, they don't. You don't. Oh, my God. Are you suggesting you think you are in love with this?" She laughs again cruelly, pointing at me.

I really do not want to hear his response. I look down at the floor.

His hand squeezes mine. "What if I am? Look, I'm sorry. I know you wanted this, but it's not going to happen. Father can't make me do this, and I won't. I'm not going to marry you. I told him last night."

"You don't think he can make it happen? You're going to take him on for this dowdy, classless little mouse? You've done well, Emily. Clearly, I underestimated you. Enjoy it while you can, because believe me, I will make your life as uncomfortable as possible. Do you really think you can make any kind with future with Gabby and humiliate me in this way?" Her tone makes it clear she is capable of what she is threatening and will not hesitate.

I want the ground to open up and swallow me. They stand, glaring at one another. Out of nowhere Serena slaps Gabriel hard across the face. The sound shatters the silence surrounding us. I look at him in shock. His cheek reddens instantly.

He drops my hand to catch hers roughly. "The first one is free, Serena," he spits out the words.

"Why? Are you going to hit me back, Gabby? I guess the apple never falls far from the tree," she simply sneers.

He visibly recoils as if she has slapped him again, his voice barely audible. "What are you talking about? I would never, ever hit a woman."

She smiles sarcastically. "Oh, yes, of course, your mother. Mummy told me about it. Our fathers are best friends, after all. Mummy explained some women just need to be kept in line. Yours was clearly one, and it seems you are much the same, Gabby."

"Your mother is on the board of a national domestic abuse

charity." He looks horrified.

"Exactly. She has seen it first-hand. Some women don't understand anything else. They just don't know how to please a man and keep him happy."

He shakes his head. His disbelief and fury are clear now, but his composure is restored. "You're disgusting, all of you. Repulsive. I guess I already knew that. If you hurt Emily or go after Emily in any way, I will destroy you."

She laughs nastily and tries to pull her hand away, which he eventually releases. She is equally furious. "How are you going to do that?"

He smiles in response. A smile which is menacing, and to be honest, more than a little frightening. "I will release the videos you sent me."

She pales slightly. "You're blagging, and anyway you told me you had deleted them. You promised you had."

His smile widens darkly. "I lied. Call it insurance. I'm sure Mummy and Daddy will be thrilled to watch their little princess go down on me and discuss her many sexual conquests male and female. Or snorting coke off the naked belly of her dealer. Freebies for sexual favours and all that."

Ouch. Was he blagging? If so, he is utterly convincing. I wonder if he would actually do it, but his current expression leaves me in no doubt this is not an idle threat.

The colour has drained from her face. "I don't believe you. You wouldn't. You wouldn't dare. Contrary to popular belief, you're not a complete bastard."

"Try me." His voice is like a whisper now, fierce and low. "Mess with Emily in any way, and you will find out, Serena. Maybe you don't know me as well as you clearly think you do."

They stare at each other for a short time. The aggression and animosity hums between them relentlessly, like a volcano about to erupt.

Serena turns her focus back to me. "Good luck if you think you can tame him." Her tone is spiteful and bitter. "You have no idea what you're getting into and what he is. What he is involved in."

"Serena." His voice is dangerously low and forbidding. He takes my hand back into his, which Serena glares at. His mood appears to have little impact on her.

"You don't scare me, Gabby. This isn't over. Do you really think you can have a normal relationship? Are you even capable? Emily will run scared when she sees you for what you really are. Trust me. She will see right through you. Just when you think things can't get any worse, I'll make sure we are all there to completely destroy you. You will have no choice but to come snivelling back to me. I will own you, Gabriel. You will have nowhere left to hide." She turns on her heels and scuttles back down the steps away from us.

I feel dizzy. My head is spinning from everything he has just said. Should I be scared? I do not know what to feel, except hurt and most of all betrayed that he would use me so callously after everything. He exhales deeply, calm and relaxed once more. I am still looking down. The tears are welling in my eyes. I know I am very close to losing it. More than anything I am utterly furious and barely able to contain my emotions. I just want to leave and get as far away from all of this as possible. As far away from him as possible.

"Emily? I'm so sorry she just did that. Emily, look at me. What's wrong?" His tone is worried.

I pull my hand away from his, glancing at him briefly, the anger and upset in me rising. "Why did you say all of that?"

"I had to threaten her with something. She can be really vindictive. Spiteful. You have no idea. It doesn't mean I would do it."

My eyes meet his. He stares at me. His expression is warm and concerned.

I can't look at him. I am shaking. Even my voice shakes. "No, not that. I get you don't want to marry her, but why imply it's about me? That was cruel. Hideously thoughtless and cruel. Even for you. You know how I feel about you."

"What? Look at me. Look at me, please."

I do as he asks and find he looks shocked, genuinely shocked and anxious.

"I meant it. Every word." He speaks more urgently. "I should have told you before now. Is it not obvious? I thought it was. Hoped it was. I guess I've been a coward. I hoped you would just know somehow."

"Told me what?"

He is making no sense whatsoever. My heart pounds in my chest like it might explode. This is awful. I just want to go and never see him again, though I am under no illusion it will help.

He touches my face with his hand. He looks earnest and a little flushed, panicked, like he is nervous. "I love you, Emily. I've fallen in love with you."

I shake my head, unable to process and understand what he is saying to me.

"It's true. I love you. This last week has been awful and lonely, really lonely, and not something I ever want to repeat. More than that, though. Like a piece of me is missing. I can't not have you with me, if you still want that, if you still want me." He looks like he is scared what I am going to say.

"You don't do relationships. Everything you said." I feel confused and wrung out. My emotions are on a volatile unpredictable rollercoaster. I am not sure I can cope with much more.

He sighs. "I know, and that was true. It's why I didn't contact you straightaway. What you said petrified me. I thought I could just move on. Fight it. Pretend it hadn't happened, but I love you. I've fallen in love with you. I can't see past it. I don't want to see past it, even though I know I'm not the best man for you. I wasn't looking for this. I've actively avoided getting involved in any kind of relationship for a long time, but I want this. I want you."

I stare at him dumbfounded.

"Christ sake, Emily. Please say something. I get it. I get it if you don't want this. If you don't want me." He searches my eyes with his, an almost desperate longing in his tone and expression.

"You love me?" I still cannot get my head around it.

He nods. "Yes, completely and hopelessly."

I look at him and all around me, trying to gather myself together. This isn't real. It can't be real.

He exhales deeply, biting his bottom lip. "Do you still love me, Emily?"

I reach my hand to his face. The colour rises in his cheeks as I press my lips to his, claiming him. "Yes, Gabriel. I love you unconditionally, and you are the right man for me."

His face breaks into a dazzling smile, the one which stops traffic. He kisses me again, like he is claiming me back.

"What happens now, Gabriel?" I have no idea.

"Move in with me. Be with me. Be part of my life. Let me be part of yours."

Ok, this cannot be real. I am dreaming, and any minute now I am going to wake up. "Move in with you?"

"Yeah, why not? Let's try it. We were doing pretty well until I fucked it up. If I fuck it up again, I will always make sure you are okay. Don't worry about anything. You can go back to University. Whatever you want, but let's at least try."

"You don't need to do that." My head is spinning.

"I know I don't need to, but I want to if you'll let me. I want you to feel secure. Safe. I want to promise you I'm not going to fuck this up, but I can't. I said I wasn't the man for you, which is true. I know I'm not great at relationships, but I love you, and I need you."

I press my lips to his again to silence him. He kisses me tenderly, slowly and sensually. Our bodies melt into one another. I have heard enough. I was already his completely. He takes my hand, and we look out across the racetrack once more as the horses start to run. Gabriel and me. Me and Gabriel. Together to face whatever comes next in our own private bubble.

The End

YOU MAY ALSO ENJOY THE FOLLOWING FROM EXTASY BOOKS INC:

Something from Nothing
Eve Morton
Release date

Excerpt

After a long sip of fortifying tea, Paige set the mug down on her dresser. She was halfway through taking out her collection of dresses when she found a beautiful gown at the back. The skirt was long and flowing, touching the carpet floor. The sleeves were long and made out of the type of fabric that would cling to her skin the moment she slid into it. The body was silky, smooth, and in midnight blue.

Was this hers? She touched its soft fabric and tried to recall a shopping endeavour with Beverly at her side or even with Luke, her ex who had the coveted black Visa card. Nothing rang a bell. She took the dress out of the closet by the hanger and admired it next to her body in the mirror. It was stunning and in her size. Yet it seemed too far away, like a graduation gown, something that she had to grow into rather than simply wear. If she put it on now, it would be too much like dress-up. She was still regarding it in the mirror when her phone chimed. She anticipated Beverly saying she forgot something.

Maybe the dress really was hers.

Paige sighed as she glimpsed the phone screen. It wasn't Beverly at all, just the reminder she'd set letting her know that rent, as ever, was due on Monday.

"Shoot."

Paige tossed the dress onto her bed and combed through her other calendar reminders. The TV news station had already paid her. There was enough in the account to absorb the rent without Beverly this month, but as she checked her remaining balance on her phone's banking app, her heart sunk at the thought of future months.

Not enough. Not by a long shot. She was going to have to start making some hard decisions about where to live now that she was by herself. While she'd considered the idea of another roommate, she also didn't want her heart to be torn in two like it was then. Living with friends was over. Living with strangers was too risky. She had to live on her own, in a much smaller place, one that didn't have memories of Beverly everywhere.

Paige spent the rest of her night sipping her tea as she looked at some apartment listings online. Everything was too expensive. Toronto was expensive. She considered moving to one of the commuter cities, but she couldn't get behind two modes of transportation just to get to work. Her job at the TV station suddenly seemed like a millstone around her neck. While at first the bright lights of the cameras and news station logo had seemed like a dream, she hadn't been promoted in two years. She wasn't a reporter, but a fact-checker for other people's stories. She'd truly believed that it would lead her somewhere good, like her degree at college would lead her somewhere good, but at twenty-five, alone, she wasn't exactly looking like a career poster child.

"Stop."

Paige stood, feeling like a small child easily distracted by bells and whistles. She didn't need to solve her job problem right now. She merely needed to cheer herself up with clothing and put the memory of Beverly behind her. After she had a night's rest, she could worry about the apartment she couldn't afford and a job that left her bored.

Paige picked up the gown and put it on without another thought. She marvelled at herself in the mirror. Nice. Her butt and breasts were especially accentuated. She added lipstick and eye shadow next, which made her face pop against the midnight blue colours. She felt like a medieval queen. She walked through her apartment, the carpet beneath her feet feeling like a cobblestone street, and the tail end of the dress floating a hair above it. This had to be Beverly's dress. Didn't she go to a renaissance fair? But, when Paige texted the image to her, asking if her liege had left something behind, Beverly sent a quick text back in the negative.

You look fantastic, but it's not mine. Halloween costume, maybe? We want to have a Halloween party, instead of a house-warming party, so I can't wait to see you in that.

Still in her get-up, Paige texted back and forth about the details of the party before Beverly's responses lapsed. Paige went back to her organizational task. When she opened the door to the Beverly's closet, she was caught off guard by mid-sized box no higher than her knees. Paige was in utter shock that Beverly had left something like that behind, especially since she'd been so meticulous. There was no writing on the side of that one, though. There were only a handful of things inside. Maybe it was supposed to be left behind? As garbage?

Paige texted a photo of the box and its open flaps to Beverly with a question mark. Not expecting anything right away, she took another look inside. It had a couple tablecloths, or maybe they were runners like for an altar. The fabric was rich and velvety, definitely not something for everyday use. There was also a deck of tarot cards and a small book that proclaimed it to be a guided resource to the mysteries of the deck. She'd seen Beverly with several decks of tarot cards before, along with some iridescent oracle ones, but she'd never seen these exact images. From what Paige could recall, this was the more traditional tarot deck, the kind that most psychics on television brandished during their 1-900 calls.

Rider-Waite, Paige read along the side of the deck and nodded with familiarity. She opened the book and confirmed what she already knew as well.

The Rider-Waite tarot deck was created in 1909 by artist Patricia Smith and A.E. Waite acting as interpreter to the symbols. These cards are to be used for divinatory purposes, rather than mere fun and games of earlier Italian tarot cards. According to . . .

Her attention flicked back to the deck. Desperate for something to remind her of Beverly, Paige shuffled them. She set out one of the tablecloths to give herself a tiny reading. She'd not done something like that before, but she'd seen Beverly toss down the cards in a cross-like pattern. She was always so tight lipped about her practice, not out of shame, but necessity, so beyond the cross pattern, Paige didn't know what else to do. The colours of the cards were nice, though, and she enjoyed thumbing through the book again to figure it all out.

She was shocked when she got to the second card, the one pressed over the first, which meant it acted as a barrier to growth. The six of cups depicted a child handing another, younger child, a golden chalice with a wonderful garden and blue sky in the background. The card, as Paige soon read, often meant that someone was stuck through memories of the past. The nice image became something juvenile to her, like the old jokes and games she'd played with Beverly.

Paige eyed the other cards, looked them up, and was equally challenged by what she'd been feeling all afternoon, and when she was really honest, all this past year. Your occupation is beyond you, the book said as it interpreted the cards. You must find something new. The last card in her reading was about money, insecurity, and the power of friends to help. The five of pentacles depicted one man on crutches hobbling his way around through a cold snowstorm.

Paige was spooked. How could all of this be so accurate? She didn't like her job. She was sad because of Beverly. She desperately needed to pay rent.

The subsequent chimes on her cell when Beverly texted back, shocked Paige out of her revelations.

Hey, Paigey. Those aren't mine. Or at least, I don't really use them. You can keep them. Considering it a parting gift.

Paige nodded at the text, even though Beverly couldn't see her. She was still baffled by this world she'd stumbled into and now wanted to rush into. She shuffled the cards again just as Beverly sent a follow up text.

Or, hey, you could start your own business! You in that dress, plus some High Priestess magick and you'll be set for life.

Paige knew it was a joke. She wanted to laugh it off and move on, but then again, their jokes had been what brought them together. She turned over the first card in the deck. It was the High Priestess dressed in a blue gown that went past her knees, over her arms, and seemed to grab the moon from the very sky and hold it as if it was its own world.

If that is not a yes from the universe, I don't know what is.

Without answering Beverly, she packed up the items she'd just discovered — only now, she put them in her bedroom.

About the Author

I live in Yorkshire, in the north of England, with my husband, four children and an assortment of animals including two giddy Labradors, a grumpy cat, three fearsome chickens, and an elderly fish called Bob. I originally grew up in Devon on the South West coast of England before moving to Yorkshire to study an Honours degree in English Literature, then a master's degree in Nineteenth Century Studies. I enjoy literature of all forms, especially romance, gothic fiction, and psychological thrillers. When I am not writing and losing myself in a romantic world, my favourite things are spending time by the sea, enjoying a glass of wine, snuggling down with a good book, painting murals, making jam, baking, and growing vegetables. I have always written and dreamed of becoming a writer. When I was a child, I would regularly write my own stories and make them into books to share with friends or take to school. I studied literature because I love to read, and I wanted to learn about other writers to improve my own writing. I have enjoyed writing contemporary, erotic, and paranormal romance for many years and am thrilled to be able to now share my stories.

Printed in Great Britain
by Amazon